OTHER BOOKS BY CHERYL LANGMESSER

PARKER MACSTUART MYSTERIES DEATH LEADS TO LIFE

BLUUD ZUUMNER

PARMALLION du NOMEL DESTRUCTION/REBIRTH

PARMALLION du NOMEL MYSTERIES ABOUND

PARKER MACSTUART MYSTERIES
THE VANISHING OF MARSHA

BY
CHERYL LANGMESSER

FORWARD

"Parker we've got to go," Mom said as she entered the library.

"I know Mom," I said and sighed as I looked at the portrait of Penelope and Sir Phillip.

"Come on Parker, everything is gonna be fine," Mom said as she took my hand then wiped her eyes.

But it wasn't fine, we were all coping because we were still here at Briargate where Penelope is. Now we have to leave which means leaving Penelope and though we're happy she's happy, it's now beginning to sink in, she's only alive on the other side and in our hearts.

The good byes would be starting, I sure wasn't looking forward to this. I went to Gerald and Sarah first, I wanted to tell them to take extra care of Grandmother, she had a weariness about her. "Gerald, Sarah please take care of yourselves and please take care and watch over Grandmother, she has a weariness about her," I said and hugged them.

"We will Miss Parker, we will," they said then we walked to Aunt Addie's and Uncle Henry's van.

We hugged Grandmother, Gerald and Sarah one more time then we got in the van and drove off. Mom cried all the way to the airport; no amount of hugging and comforting words could help her. "Mom I'm sorry!" I cried and started sobbing.

"Parker stop it! Please stop it! It's not your fault! Please baby stop blamin' yourself!" Mom cried.

"I thought I had stopped blamin' myself. I did as long as we were there," I said and wiped my eyes, then Dom bundled me up.

Dom held me all the way to the airport; by the time we parked Mom and I finally stopped blubbering. We entered the terminal, all heads turned to look at us, the tall family and the cellphones came out. Then they zeroed in on Mom and I, the big women, eyes bloodshot from crying with runny noses, I'm sure they thought we were on drugs. We said good bye to Aunt Addie and Uncle Henry, then went through security and we were on our way home.

The start of our flight was smooth, I hadn't had an unsettling experience since Hockey and Plute, well that all changed. We had been in the air for fifteen minutes when I zoned out. It was a bright sunny day; I had no idea where I was at or what I was looking at. It felt as if I was looking at wherever and whatever from above; this was a new for me. I heard a massive crashing noise and then I saw a fireball rise up into the air. Then the scene shifted, I saw bars as on a prison cell and lurking in the deep shadows was a form.

I came back with a jolt luckily we hit some turbulence which covered up my arrival. "Parker what happened?" Mom asked as I squeezed her hand.

"I don't know. I've had only pleasant experiences since the Hockey and Flute episode but this one was unsettling. It's a bright sunny day; I have no idea where I'm at but it felt familiar at the same time. I felt as if I was hovering above lookin' down on the scene. There was a horrible crashing noise then there was a huge fireball that rose up into the air. Then the scene shifted and I saw what looked to be a door to a prison cell, behind the door in the deep shadows was a form," I said.

"Parker what do you think it means?" Mom asked.

"I don't know, I actually thought I was gonna see Penelope and Sir Phillip. But when I heard the crash, it didn't sound like anything that would be in Sir Phillip's time. It really sounded as if vehicles crashed and exploded."

"Well it seems to me that someone is tryin' to show you something but why go about it this way? All I hope is it's not something bad," Mom said and squeezed my hand.

"I hope so too," I said and squeezed back but I had a bad feeling, a very bad feeling about this.

The rest of the flight was uneventful without any more experiences and we were soon down on the ground. We left the plane and were heading to get our luggage, as we were coming out of the tunnel/hallway, Dad was the first one to see the vultures as he called them, the reporters were here!

"Will, Cora! Will, Cora! How's it feel to be home?" they yelled and shoved cameras and microphones in Mom's and Dad's face. The people starting to crowd around us pulled out their cellphones, they were ready for footage to post online.

"Parker, Parker how do you feel about losin' your sister?" one of the reporters asked, that stopped us in our tracks.

"How does it make me feel? What a stupid question you stupid fool!" I snarled and they backed up.

I was furious! I started toward them eyes blazing with hatred, nostrils flared. When this happens everyone that knows me, knows to give me plenty of space. Thoughts of that terrible day and attack were on my mind, then all of a sudden Sir Phillip, Martin and Robert appeared! **"How dare you ask this fine young lady and her family these ignorant and unwanted questions!"** they bellowed and tore into them.

In the ensuing melee Penelope appeared briefly, "Get out of here now!" she disappeared as quickly as she appeared. We quickly made our way to the luggage carousel, grabbed our luggage and left the terminal. As soon as we were in the parking lot and in our van Sir Phillip, Martin and Robert disappeared leaving everyone bloody, shaken and wondering what just happened.

We didn't say anything until we were out of sight of the airport. "Parker what happened?" Dad asked.

"I don't know, shoot yes I do. When that jerk asked me how I felt, I was slammed with guilt. I was thinkin' about Penelope and how Sir Phillip, Martin and Robert rushed to protect us, that's when they appeared," I said.

"Well I for one am glad you had those thoughts and they came. Damn dirty bastards," Dad snarled.

"I am too, maybe they'll leave us alone," the quads said.

"We can only hope," Mom said.

"God I hope so, I'm really tired of it, really tired of it," I said and wiped my eyes.

"Parker are you ready to pick up Marco?" Mom asked.

"I won't be able to, he's gone," Mom and Dad cut me off.

"What do you mean, he's gone?" they asked with disbelief.

"Marsh's dad opened the cage and let Marco out, he got outside then a dog ate him. Poor old Marsh is beside herself, it's not even her fault and I don't know how to tell her or even if I should tell her. So I'll have to hug her while she apologizes for something she didn't even do," I said. My family sighed and shook their heads, they finally understood what I had been telling them all along, Marsh's dad doesn't like me.

"Parker, I'm so sorry. I'm sorry we didn't believe you when you said Quinn didn't like you. But why?" Mom asked.

"Thanks Mom, thanks all of you. I think, well I'm pretty sure he doesn't like me because he called me a liar and said I was a fake. Well I told him he didn't know what he was talkin' about. Then I told him something very personal, oh like the name of his latest mistress and asked if he wanted me to continue with the names of the others," I said and my family gasped.

"I heard rumors about him carrying on for years," Mom said.

"That damned bastard why didn't you say something?" Dad asked.

"She did, the quads and I paid him a visit. Since you work with him we didn't want to cause problems, so we took care of it," Mom said and gave Dad a look and he let it drop.

"Parker what happened to Marco?" the quads asked.

"Marco let me know what happened a week ago. He told me that Marsh loved him to pieces, gave him a kiss and put him in his cage and made sure the door was secure. This happened just a couple of days after we left, it took him that long to make contact. He's livin' with, are you ready for it, Penelope and Sir Phillip," I said.

"You're kiddin' me?" everyone said and started laughing.

"Are you ready? Do you want one of us to come with you?" Mom asked.

"Yeah I'm ready. Thanks for the offer but I'll go by myself," I said as we turned onto Marsha's street. The ugly aura was still there and uglier than before.

"I was hopin' that ugly aura would be gone but it's worse now than when we left. I thought it was the flu but now I'm not sure what it is," I said and Dad pulled in the driveway.

Marsh came out, followed closely be her brothers and behind them were her parents. "God damn I really don't want to talk to him, especially after what you just told us. Damn, damn, double damn; all I want to do is get us home so we can just take a deep breath and collect ourselves. Well let's get this over with," Dad said none to thrilled with having to make small talk.

Mom, Dad and the quads got a hug and a handshake from Marsh and her entire family. I got a hug from Marsh; the others wouldn't hug me or shake my hand if their lives depended on it. I went with Marsh as the others went inside as soon as we were alone in the backyard the crying and apologizing started. While I was comforting Marsh, I saw the same vision I had on the plane. "Marsh it's okay, don't worry about it you didn't do anything so it's not your fault. Marco was an escape artist," I said. I lied then apologized to Marco for lying, I told him I didn't want to tell her, her dad did it and he understood.

"Parker, thank you for forgiving me! I'll make it up to you, I promise!" Marsh cried.

"Marsh you don't have to, please don't worry about it. Marsh are you guys gonna go anywhere for the holiday?" I asked.

"Yeah, we are, we're leavin' next Friday right after I get home from school. Why?" Marsh asked.

"I was just wondering if you wanted to come over and stay the weekend. But we'll do it another time, so no worries. Come on let's get back," I said.

"Parker I'm really glad you're back and I'm very sorry about Penelope. If you ever need to talk about anything, I'll be here for you," Marsh said.

"Thanks Marsh, one day we'll have a long talk about it, but not right now, it hurts too bad," I said and wiped my eyes.

"Parker I understand, when you're ready to talk I'll listen," Marsh said and squeezed my hand then we walked back to her house.

We visited for a few more minutes, then Marsh and her family walked us to our van, much to the relief of her father. "Have fun on your long weekend, please be careful and safe," I said then we pulled out of their driveway and headed for home.

When we got into the van I settled back and I was on a road or near a road or above a road. I had no clue where I was at, it felt familiar but I just couldn't get my bearings. Once again I could hear a great crashing sound, once again I saw the great ball of fire as well as the hidden from in the prison cell. I came back and sucked in a great breath of air.

"Parker!" Mom and Dad exclaimed.

"I'm fine, I was there again. Mom, Dad I don't know where I'm at but it feels familiar. I feel as if I'm above everything. I've never had anything like this before," I said and sighed.

"Do you have someone you can talk to? Crap what a question," Dad said and shook his head.

"Dad that's alright and yeah I have a couple of people I can talk to. I've talked to them since I was two," I said.

"Oh I remember them; do you think they'll be able to help you?" Dad asked.

"Yeah they should but I'm dreading the answer I'll get. I really do believe this has got to do with Marsh and her family," I said and fell silent.

We didn't say anything else the entire way home. I was able to talk to my friends and they confirmed my worst fears. To make a very long painful story short, I told Marsh and her family what I saw. Marsh believed me, her grandfather did too, her mom didn't want to but I could tell she did but her father, forget it. He would do anything to prove me wrong, he hated me and hated my friendship with Marsh. Mom and Dad even talked to Quinn but it didn't do any good, matter of fact I think it made it worse.

The long holiday weekend was here, my stomach was in knots. The aura around Marsh was ugly and swirling, I told Marsh again to be careful and what I've seen and when it would start. I hugged her hard, we were in tears.

I worried and paced all night long, at 9:30 p.m., without any news I was beginning to think I was wrong and I was starting to relax. The phone rang and there was loud knocking on the door, my worst fears came true and all hell broke loose.

CHAPTER ONE
TREASURES TO BE SOLD

I saw Parker on Friday; she was worried sick about me and my family. "Marsh please," Parker said.

"Parker I know. I talked to Mom and Dad, I told them you said to leave just five minutes later. Parker he just looked at me he doesn't believe you!" I cried.

"I know Marsh, I know. Marsh please try and leave five minutes later! If you can't please buckle in, please get your family to buckle in! Please Marsh promise me you'll buckle in and have your family buckle in!" Parker stressed.

"I promise Parker! I promise!" I cried and we hugged then we had to go our separate ways.

Parker ran out of school to see me getting in my van. My dad saw Parker, he pulled out so fast I fell into the van and the door slammed shut, almost on my legs.

"Marsh buckle in!" Parker yelled.

"Parker I promise I'll buckle in!" I cried.

I was in the back with Grandfather, "Dad please slow down! Five minutes, what's five minutes, please so down!" I cried but he wouldn't, in fact he sped up.

"I'm gonna show you two that bitch you call a friend is full of shit!" Dad yelled and shot me a look; he had a crazed look on his face that scared me more than his crazy driving.

"Quentin stop it, what's wrong with you? Parker is a very nice girl," Grandfather said.

"Go to hell old man," Dad snarled and shot Grandfather a nasty look.

"So be it, I know I made the correct decision," Grandfather said and fell silent, then patted my hand.

"Marsha it's gonna be alright, you'll see. Just buckle and hang on to me," Grandfather said, he pulled my seatbelt tight, adjusted his and held me tight.

My dad stopped and picked up my brothers, then stopped to pick up Mom. Dad was driving like a mad man, scaring everyone in the van. "Dad please slow down!" I cried and Grandfather bundled me up.

"Quentin slow down you're scarin' Marsha!" Grandfather barked.

"Grandfather we're gettin' close to the time and place that Parker told me about," I said.

"Marsha dear I know she told me too. Just hold on to me and shut your eyes," Grandfather said and squeezed.

The time and the place was here, Dad looked at me in the review mirror. "I told you she's wrong!" I opened my eyes, they widened; at the same time both Mom and I screamed.

We crossed the centerline in the road, we jerked hard and missed the semi. Then we jerked back and clipped the back end of a cargo van which sent us into the first semi. From that we were pushed out and away and hit another semi head on. The sound of crashing and screaming blended together and became one, this was the last sound I heard for quite a while.

As soon as Quinn opened his eyes on the other side he said, "Dirty bitch I'll get you for this."

A woman appeared before him, "I can help you with that. Would you still do it if it means hurting your daughter?" the woman asked.

"Yes, I don't care if it hurts that brat, I never wanted her anyway. I just want to get even with that tall bitch. Do you boys want to join me?" Quinn asked.

"No we might have followed you in other things but this time we want no part of it," Quinn Jr. said.

"So be it, you're nothin' but a bunch of sniveling cowards," Quinn Sr. said.

"Then come with me," the woman said and held out her hand. He took it without giving any thought to Andy; his wife and his sons and he simply walked off.

"Marsh, Marsh can you hear me? Marsh it's me Parker."

Her voice sounded so far away, I was so tired, I just couldn't go to her voice. "Come on Marsh you've got to fight! Fight, do you hear me fight!" Parker ordered.

There was so much power in her voice that I felt compelled to go to her. "Alright Parker, I'm comin'," I said weakly and started toward her.

Fast forward three years, I don't know where they went but I'm sure glad they're behind me. Now if I had this meeting with Trevor behind me, I'd be a very happy girl and I walked into his office.

We made small talk, we always do, then down to business. "Beautiful, beautiful, just beautiful. This is the most beautiful piece yet. Marsha where did you find these treasures?" Trevor asked.

"They were in my grandfather's house, well now it's my house, too bad it came to me this way," and I fell silent; then continued, "Sorry about that, well any way there's so much more where this came from. Some of them I'd like to donate to the museum others I'll keep or sell. Will you help me sort through them?" I asked.

"I'd love to. I'm busy all this week but if you're agreeable to next week, I'll be glad to help. I can't wait to see what you have," Trevor said and I just didn't like the sound of that.

"Next week is fine. I'll be able to get several rooms ready," I said and left the office. I really was glad to get out of that office. Something comes over that man whenever he sees a nice piece and I shuddered.

I drove the nearly sixty miles to my grandfather's house; I mean my house, one of these days that will feel right to say but not today. So anyway I drove to Cinder Falls it's so beautiful here, the land is green and rolls from hill to hill. The farmer's lands were separated from each other by trees and rock fences. There wasn't anything grown here but lush grasses where some dairy cattle, a few sheep and horses grazed. The land in and around the small community of Cinder Falls had been in the families since they arrived here in the late 1500's. It seemed to be set down in stone that the property would pass within the family from generation to generation.

Since my entire family was taken away from me at fifteen in a terrible accident, that could have easily been prevented, well anyway at that tender age I became the sole beneficiary of my Grandfather's estate. After Grandfather recovered and was allowed to come home, he told me what he meant about making the right decision. He cut Dad and my brothers out of his will; only Mom and I were the beneficiaries, now that Mom was gone I was the only one. He wouldn't tell me why and what they did, but it must have been heinous.

Had it not been for Parker, her family and Grandfather I would have gone crazy with grief and anger with my father for the accident that took my beloved mother and brothers from me.

I lived with Grandfather until his death two years later, ultimately from the injuries he received during the accident. So on my seventeenth birthday, Grandfather went to the other side as Parker calls it and that's one birthday I'd like to forget. All I can say is thank god for Parker and her family, had it not been for them I would have been placed in a foster home. At eighteen I received the entire estate as its owner instead of being held in a trust and managed for me by a team of lawyers.

I started college that fall I was so sad because Grandfather wasn't there. We had my first day of college all planned out years in advance. I had hoped he'd be there when I graduated as a forensic anthropologist, now he would only be with me in spirit. It will be a bitter sweet day.

So now that I'm alone in this huge house I'm going to get rid of some of the things that I couldn't stand. Grandfather had bought and inherited pieces that were so ugly it could crackle the paint on the walls! On the other hand there were some magnificent and beautiful pieces. I was going to keep the pieces that were special to me and those that have been in the family for centuries. The only items that Trevor was going to look at were the ones that came into the family by marriage or were purchased over the years. I would donate all the proceeds from these items to my favorite museum and to my high school.

I had been slowly going through these vast treasures and I'm telling you some of these so-called treasures were nothing but junk and garbage! There were old pieces of papers, scraps of fabric, cracked buttons, shards of glass, nails, bits of metal and the list of junk just went on. During one weekend, I threw out sixty large black garbage bags of the items listed above!

I had cleaned out the basement and I was down doing some laundry when I dropped some change, off it rolled and the chase was on! It rolled behind the wall thanks to a hole. I knelt down and fished around with a hanger and a small door popped open!

Inside this little compartment was a box wrapped in old brown paper. I pulled it out and shook it. There was something solid in it. I opened up and there was an envelope with my name on it, this letter was from Grandfather.

"My dearest Marsha, if you have found this burn it. I could never bring myself to do it, I wasn't strong enough and it had a powerful hold on me. If you go against my advice and read them have the bible on your right and a crucifix on your left."

"These books were said to be the cause of your great, great, great, great aunts we'll just call her your Aunt Gracie's madness. They said the books also caused the death of several in our family and several people in a little town called Popsville."

"It all started in the fall of 1891 when Aunt Gracie had a visitor, a nice young woman from what I've heard. The woman named Rosy came to Aunt Gracie's house right after her husband died and her young twin sons almost died. She had answered an advertisement placed by Aunt Gracie's sister to do housework and the general care and upkeep of the house while Gracie recovered."

"After Aunt Gracie's husband's death she wasn't the same, she let her sister take her children because she wasn't fit to do so. When Aunt Gracie's housekeep/ visitor/friend left she left her journal behind, the other journal is your aunt's rantings. Please Marsha, I beg you not to read these insanities. Love Grandfather."

"Oh Grandfather how I wish you were here! But you don't have anything to worry about, but then again you always did worry too much," I said, placed the books back in the box; took them to the library and put them in the desk.

Between my studies and trying to get things ready for Trevor the week flew by; all thoughts of the books vanished. I was so busy with all my studies and searching for treasures I didn't get nearly as many items together as I wanted to.

"Trevor I'm sorry I wasn't able to get more together," I apologized yet again.

"Marsha you don't have to apologize. I understand and this trip wasn't for naught. These are fabulous pieces and will fetch a fair price for you," Trevor said rubbing his hands greedily along the spine of a book from 1776.

"Trevor do you want to come back next Friday?" I asked.

"I'd love to but I'm gonna be out of town on a buying trip. How about the Saturday after that is that okay with you?" Trevor asked.

"That's fine with me. That will give me some more time to get things together," I said and helped him load the treasures into his van.

I watched him drive off and went back into the house and grabbed the phone on the last ring, "Hello?"

"Hey Parker! What's up?" I asked.

"No I'm not really busy, just goin' through some of the stuff in the house. Would you like to come over and we can goof around like when we were little kids?" I asked.

"Sure Friday would be great. We can drive to school together, so I'll come pick you up," I said.

Parker and I have always been close, we've known each other since we were six months old; I'm five days older than she is. We became even closer after Penelope disappeared. Parker was never able to have the close relationship with her sister when they were living under the same roof and that hurt her so very much. And if her sister's disappearance wasn't bad enough I even managed to lose her pet rat Marco; whom she loved like family. Lord almighty I sure don't know how it happened but happen it did. I didn't think Parker would ever forgive me, but she did. I'm sure most people would have walked away and mourned the loss of their sister in private and never talked to me again.

And then when I learned what really happened to Marco, I nearly fainted. Crud when Momma Cora, that's what I've always called Parker's mother, told me what really happened to Marco, well I couldn't believe it! I knew my dad didn't like Parker but to do this to a poor innocent, cute rat, well it cut clear to my core. I cried and apologized and cried and apologized some more. I'm still surprised Parker wants to be friends with me.

I picked Parker up early Friday morning and I do mean early, before 5:30 a.m. Since we both had early classes, they started at 7:00 a.m. and a pretty long drive, it was a very early wake up call. She threw her bag in the back seat, gave me a hug and said, "Man am I glad we have just once class today. I'm pooped!" Parker exclaimed.

"Me too! This has been a very busy week. I'm really glad to have a three-day weekend," I said.

"Marsh what's botherin' you? You seem a little on edge," Parker said.

"I don't know. I'm sure it's nothin', but I feel as if Trevor is short changin' me or if he isn't he's goin' to. It just bothers me," I replied.

"Do you want me to meet him some time?" Parker asked.

"That might not be a bad idea. He'll be at the house next weekend. What are doin' then?" I asked.

"Oh shoot Marsh I can't. We've got this family thing, I'm sorry," Parker replied.

"Parker don't worry about it. There will be a lot of times in the future. Ooh, you know what? I can call him and cancel and re-schedule when you can be there!" I said excitedly.

"Well if you want to but I don't want to screw things up for you. Before you cancel check his schedule and if he's flexible then I'll be there and check him out," Parker replied.

"Sounds good to me. He'll be very flexible, his eyes glaze over every time I show him a piece," I said.

The conversation soon turned from Trevor to more important things, girl talk and the miles rolled by; soon we were in the parking lot. "Boy time flies when you're havin' fun," I said.

"Boy that's for sure. See you after class," Parker said.

"See you later," I said and off we went to our classes.

"Parker, I'm sorry but the professor just couldn't shut up," I said.

"Marsh don't worry about it. You're only five minutes late. Now, let's go get something to eat. I'm starving!" Parker said as her stomach let out a huge gurgle.

As we were eating I had the strangest feeling we were being watched and I shuddered. "Parker what do you feel?" I asked.

"Your grandfather is sittin' in the booth next to you and one behind. He says hi. Hi Mr. Larkwood. You're lookin' good," Parker said and waved.

"Parker! What are you doin'? There's no one there," I turned around there sat Grandfather.

"Grandfather," I squeaked. He smiled and then he was gone with the ringing of the bell on the diner door.

"Oh poo, Grandfather, oh poo," I said and hit the table with disgust.

"Marsh, stop, he'll be back. He's always around you, all you have to do is just relax and let everything else fall away," Parker said.

"Oh Parker I know but it's hard for me and so easy for you," I said and sighed.

"Like I said, don't worry about it," Parker said and threw her straw wrapper at me and we both started to laugh.

"Come on let's go and start our long weekend," I said.

"That sounds good to me," Parker replied.

"Parker is Grandfather around?" I asked.

"No he isn't. But there's a slight fog by you and I can't penetrate it. It's gone. You know that's the first time that's ever happened. Oh well I'll figure it out," Parker said.

"Parker when you're twenty-one you'll know everything about what you can do right?" I asked.

"So I've been told. I just can't wrap my head around that concept. Maybe what they mean is with the fog that I can't penetrate. Maybe if I was older then I'd know how to do it. But you know I'm just not gonna worry about it," Parker said and I knew she would stew about this for quite a while.

We had only been on the road for ten minutes when Parker let out a gasp, grabbed the arm rest on her right and the arm rest in the middle between us. "Parker! What's the matter?" I asked frantically and pulled the car over.

"Marsh, there's something bad comin' your way. It's just a blackness around you. It could be just a slight illness or a period of bad grades or something that's just slightly odd," Parker said.

"Are you sure you're alright? Are you tellin' me everything?" I asked.

"Yeah I'm fine and yes I told you everything," Parker said.

For the first time in my life I lied to Marsh. She didn't need to know what I saw around her which was deception, lies and death

We pulled up in front of the house and I had to stifle the shudder that was creeping up on me. I couldn't figure out how and why Marsh couldn't feel this, it was extremely oppressive. Then Mr. Larkwood appeared and the feeling vanished. Whatever was here, it did not like or feared Mr. Larkwood.

"Well come on Parker let's get in and you can get settled," I said.
"Sounds good to me. Come on," Parker said. We linked arms and skipped into the house like we did when we were small kids.

CHAPTER TWO
UNWELCOME VISITOR

"Parker which room do you want? The one overlooking the front yard or one of the back rooms overlooking the pond?" I asked.

"Well how about one that's close to yours overlooking the pond," Parker said.

"I was hopin' you'd pick that one, I already have it fixed up for you," I said and we both giggled.

As we were heading for the stairs to get to our rooms, I noticed Parker looking at the door to the library and before I could ask her about it, Parker asked, "Marsh have you noticed anything strange in the house?"

"Not really, why?" I asked.

"Because there was a woman standing by the door. She has light brown hair pulled up in a bun. She has very smooth white skin, no blemishes, freckles and bright green eyes. She was dressed in a long black skirt and a white blouse that was buttoned at the neck. It was one of those with the frilly collars like you see in a lot of pictures from right around the turn of the century. She had on long sleeves, a dark shawl and a party mask," Parker said.

"Who is it? How could you tell what she looked like if she had a mask on?" I asked.

"I don't know who she is, she's not tellin' me, but she definitely seems cold. It was only a half mask that's how I could see most of her face," Parker said.

"Well I wonder who it is and why she's here," I said.

"I don't know but she's gone now. I wouldn't worry about it because your grandfather is around keepin' an eye on things. I think it's someone who's a little upset with you for goin' through their things," Parker said; since that sounded plausible to me I let it go and we went upstairs.

The rest of the day was quiet, we didn't have any more uninvited guests and we found several very interesting pieces. We would have found more but Parker did a reading on each one at my insistence of course!

We found a beautiful broach from the early 1800's, a few very old bibles, a rolled-up map of the town of Popsville from 1799 and a portrait of Mayor Hornbark from the year 1889, he was the mayor of Cinder Falls.

"You know Parker if I can find out if the mayor has any descendants I'm gonna contact them, maybe they'd like the portrait. How did we end up with it?" I asked.

"Well they might, it was just before the affair started. He was in love with your many great Aunt Gracie. Her love for him was all consuming until his wife came to see your aunt," Parker said.

"Wow you mean she was in love with a married man! Oh what a scandal that must have been. Did she know he was married from the beginning? What happened?" I asked.

"Yeah she did matter of fact she was the one who pursued him," Parker said and I nearly fell over.

"You're kiddin' me. Well she seems a little loose," I said.

"She kept that side of her personality very well hidden. When everyone found out about the affair they all thought it was the mayor's fault. So of course the mayor was blamed for everything; from crop failure to dry wells. Not that he wasn't guilty but if she wouldn't have pursued him and thrown herself at him, he never would have searched her out," Parker said.

"Talk about skeletons in your closet," I said.

"Oh it gets better. Gracie's father was the town doctor and had to be locked up in his cellar until he calmed down. The mayor's father-in-law was a prominent lawyer and was ready to kill the mayor, so he had to be watched day and night. They had to release the doctor because his patients needed him, so the doctor and the father-in-law were both escorted around day and night until the mayor was persuaded to resign and leave town," Parker said.

"Where did he go?" I asked.

"Well everyone thought he went west to Illinois to stay with his widowed sister so he could help run her place. She waited for a month and when he didn't show up she sent him a letter. She waited for another month and then she sent a letter to the sheriff."

"The sheriff went to the mayor's house and what he found there sickened him. The mayor's wife and children had been butchered, throats slit, stomachs cut open and organs flung around the house. This was the worst crime he had ever seen but it seemed familiar and then he remembered the Ripper murders," and I cut Parker off.

"You've got to be kiddin' me!" I exclaimed.

"Nope I'm not. It was very similar. To the end of his days the sheriff said this was the worst sight he had ever seen, even worse than the makeshift military hospital his house became durin' the Civil War when he was just a wee lad," Parker said.

"Why did he kill his family?" I asked.

"He didn't, they all thought he did but he left a note. He told them who killed his family and he pinned the note to his chest, put the noose around his neck and spurred his horse. When they found his body only part of the note remained. The murderer was never found and it still remains a mystery to this day," Parker said.

"Well do you know if it was Jack the Ripper who did this?" I asked.

"No it wasn't, but I can't see the killer at all. The harder I look the less I see and feel. So for right now this will stay unsolved. Can we talk about something else; this is really startin' to bother me," Parker said.

"Okay no more talk of it," I said. I knew that this must really be bothering Parker otherwise she would continue reading.

"Parker when you says it bothers you, do you mean physically or mentally?" I asked.

"Both, most of the time. Sometimes it's more mental sometimes it's more physical. When the physical happens I can sometimes bleed from wounds. But most of the times I just get red, raised welts where the wounds are and they burn; that's just a little unpleasant," Parker said.

"God Parker I didn't realize that! Is everyone like that?" I asked.

"No as far as I know I'm the only one. Every person that I've been to agrees that mine is a rare talent and a true one. I'm sure it nearly killed some of these skeptics to say that I'm officially genuine. I could have told them that without havin' to go through the battery of tests they put me through, but they needed proof," Parker said.

"Since you're on the books as genuine what does that mean for you?" I asked.

"Well for one when there's a case that can't be solved I'm called in. The first thing they have me do is when the suspects are called in I sit outside the interview room; on three of those occasions they had the killer. In the past three months I've been called for ten different unsolved cases. Mom finally had to put a stop to it because my grades were startin' to suffer. I'm tellin' you that was a scene in our house," Parker said.

"Parker that's terrible, aren't there any others they can contact?" I asked.

"From what I've been told the others aren't as clear as I am. They see little snippets and give out clues that are hard to figure out. But I get the entire picture in color and in its entirety. I tell you some of the things I've seen would make a grown man scream. So most of the time I tune everything out," Parker said.

"You know I was always jealous of your abilities and I wanted them, but after what you've told me, I don't want them anymore," I said.

"You know Marsh when I was younger; I wanted to get rid of them in the worst way, but not so now. When I'm able to help people it makes all the intrusions worth it," Parker said and yawned which caused me to yawn.

"Oh this is ridiculous, come on let's go to bed," I said and yawned again.

"You won't get any arguments out of me," Parker said, yawned and shook her head.

Once in my room and settled into bed all traces of being tired went away, I was wide awake. I laid there and looked at the ceiling and the shadows on it. These shadows were from the curtains that were blowing because I had the windows open.

I tossed and turned for a few minutes when I finally found a comfy spot and fell asleep. I woke up with a start and checked the time, 11:42 p.m., I rolled over got comfortable and went back to sleep.

Yet again I woke with a start and was surprised that my blankets had been pulled off of me and over the foot board.

I got up and pulled my blankets up. I turned around because I felt something behind me and I thought it was Parker, but there wasn't anyone there. "Great, just great remind me to never have Parker tell me things. Get a grip."

Back to bed, more tossing and turning and finally back to sleep. Once again I woke up but this time I thought I heard something and then I noticed my blankets were once again off and over the foot board.

I fixed the blankets and went to the bathroom. When I came out I thought I saw movement in the shadows in the corner next to my bed. The longer I stood there the more the shadow formed and when it stepped out of the corner I let out a yell and took off.

"Parker!" I yelled and ran out of my room.

"Parker! Parker!" I yelled and almost ran into her.

"Marsh what's the matter? Are you alright?" Parker asked with alarm.

"I'm alright, I think. There's something in my room. It came out of the shadows and something kept pullin' my blankets off me," I said.

"Let me go check it out. You stay here," Parker said and off she went.

I stood in the hallway and the minutes ticked by. When Parker didn't come out after five minutes I went to go into my room and found the door locked.

"Parker are you alright?" I asked and jiggled the door knob.

"Parker answer me! Come on open the door!" I yelled and pounded on the door, but still no answer.

I wasn't going to wait anymore. I knew there were keys in Grandfather's room. I turned and started to run. I ran to Grandfather's room and that stupid door was stuck yet again. "Crud come on!" I yelled at the door.

"Marsh, I'm fine," Parker said as she walked up behind me; I nearly jumped off the floor!

"Parker! Are you sure you're okay?" I asked.

"Yeah I'm sure. Come on let's go downstairs to the kitchen and I'll fill you in," Parker said.

CHAPTER THREE
EVIL BEGINS

Parker led me to the kitchen, sat me down and poured us two glasses of milk. "First off I still don't know who the woman is, but she's the one I saw at the library door. Your grandfather was there when I went in."

"He said he'd try to keep her away, but he doesn't know who she is. He said she's been hangin' around for several months always hangin' in and around the library."

"I told him I'll figure out who it is even if it takes me the rest of my life. Once I find out who it is I'll send her away and he seemed a little more at ease. She's proving to be a little difficult but she doesn't know me and how persistent I can be. It might take me awhile but I'll figure it out. Marsh if you want you can stay with us," Parker said.

"Is it that bad? Parker are you sure you're tellin' me everything?" I asked.

"No it's not that bad and yes I'm tellin' you the truth and everything. It can be upsetting when you start to see supernatural happenings. Since you're alone and so busy maybe it would be better if you'd stay with us until this is all sorted out," Parker said.

"Let me think about it and I'll let you know once the weekend is over. You're still gonna stay here aren't you?" I asked.

"Sure why wouldn't I? I might even be able to get some clues as to who your visitor is, if you still want me to," Parker said.

"Yeah I still want you to find out who it is. Why is she here now?" I asked.

"I'm not sure but my theory is that she was afraid of your grandfather for some reason. And as he weakened and then when he passed she was able to get in. She's still able to get around him because he's still very weak."

"I'm gonna try and contact some of the others that have lived here maybe they can shed some light on this mystery. Before I start I want to get out of the house for a couple of hours, just to clear my head," Parker said.

"Sounds good to me, so when do you want to go?" I asked.

"Well I want to get some more sleep; we'll stay together, so nothin' will happen. Maybe we could leave around six and go into town and eat breakfast. Then we can come back and I'll be fresh," Parker said.

"Sounds like a plan to me," I said as we started back to Parker's room.

As soon as my head hit the pillow I was asleep and this time I slept through the rest of the night. When I woke up, it was 5:30 and the rain was coming down in buckets. Parker was dressed and standing in front of the window with her hands behind her back, her long, thick blue/black hair touching her hands. She is an imposing figure, standing there like she is; it almost seems she's guarding this room, daring anything to pass her way. I have always felt safe and secure when Parker is with me.

"Do you still want to go?" I asked.

"Yeah, I need to clear my thoughts. Come on let's get your stuff and go," Parker replied.

We drove down to Annie's Diner, which is about ten miles from my house. Parker was very quiet and didn't seem like her old self. She had been out of sorts since last night's episode but she would never admit it.

"Marsha, Parker, it's so good to see you again. How are you?" Annie Princeton the 3rd asked.

"We're fine Annie, how are you?" I asked.

"I'm fine, have you decided?" Annie asked.

"Yeah we have, can we get the special?" I asked and watched her walk off.

"I wonder if she'll name her daughter Annie?" Parker asked.

"I didn't know she was pregnant," I replied stupidly.

"Yeah she is and she doesn't know it yet. Marsh did I tell you that I figured out who Jack the Ripper is?" Parker asked.

I looked at Parker as if she had lost her mind but then again when Parker says things like she just did there was a reason behind it. "No you didn't, why?" I asked.

"Remember when I said the sheriff thought the murders were similar to the Ripper murders?" she asked.

"Yeah I do, but are you, Parker," I stammered.

"That's exactly what I'm tellin' you. The mayor's family was killed by the same person that killed in White Chapel. I didn't tell you before because I didn't want to upset you any more than you already were. The name of Jack the Ripper is Rosy Whipnickly," Parker said and I sucked in a breath of air.

"I also have to tell you that when I say they were killed by the same person; they were but they weren't. The Rosy who killed the mayor's family wasn't the Rosy that killed in White Chapel. The White Chapel Rosy was driven by hatred. The White Chapel Rosy didn't physically kill the mayor's family. The spirit of Rosy when she was killin' took over the person I can't see," Parker said.

"You're kiddin' me; this is awfully hard to believe that a spirit of someone that went nuts could somehow possess another person. Well why did Rosy kill in London?" I asked.

"She killed in White Chapel because her father got an STD from a prostitute. He gave it to her mother and her mother died a horrible death. This ate at Rosy until she couldn't control her feelings and she snapped. She killed every one she saw her father with and that was a lot of women. Once she killed them her hatred was spent and she left the country. Like I said she didn't kill the mayor's family and I still don't know who did it but it has something to do with the woman in your house," Parker said.

I was going to say something but our food came. The restaurant was filling up so we just sat in silence for several minutes and then I broke the silence. "Parker do you want to go straight home?"

"No can we take a ride to the cemetery?" Parker asked.

"Sure," I said and I could see Parker tense up and then it passed as quickly as it came.

We drove the fifteen miles to St. Bede's and entered through the ornate wrought iron gates. "Marsh go straight and then take the right lane. When you get to the winged horse go left," Parker said and shut her eyes.

I came to the horse made my turn and looked at Parker who seemed to be asleep. "Marsh go to the end of the road, turn right, then left and stop at the mausoleum with the roses made out of quartz above the door," Parker said.

"Parker we're here," I said then continued, "Are you alright?"

"Yeah I'm fine. I just need to go talk to Nanna for a few minutes. Come on," Parker said.

"Are you sure?" I asked.

"Yeah, it's not a problem. I want you to come in with me," Parker said and led the way.

Parker walked up to her great-grandmother's, Father Will's grandmother's sarcophagus and knelt down. "Hi Nanna, how are you today? You remember Marsh don't you? Nanna says hi," Parker said.

"Hi, how are you?" I asked.

"Nanna says hi and thank you for askin'," Parker said. She fell silent and for the next several minutes she sat there, every once in a while she'd smile or chuckle softly or shrug. She stood up put her fingers to her lips and then touched her great-grandmother's name and then walked out of the mausoleum.

"Marsh I want you to stay with me for a few days. I don't want you in that house alone. You are in jeopardy. I won't take no for an answer," Parker stressed.

"But why? Did your great-grandmother say something?" I asked.

"No. It's just something that I'm feelin', nothin' I can put my finger on. So after we make our next stop we'll go back to your house, pack up and we're goin' home. Marsh I'll tell you right now you're in danger. If I can keep you safe for the next couple of weeks then the danger is over," Parker said.

"From what? Why now? Who's threatening me? Is it safe to be in my house?" I asked frantically.

"It's safe in the house for now because your grandfather, my Nanna and several others will be there to protect you. It's happening now because your grandfather is dead and you found something evil. When we make our last stop hopefully I'll know who or what it is," Parker said and started for the car, she turned around and said, "I'm gonna drive. I know I upset you and I'm sorry for that, but I always feel it's best to get to the point and not hide the truth."

"Parker I know and thank you, it's just very hard to grasp. Where are we goin' anyway?" I asked.

"We're gonna pay a visit to the mayor's wife and kids. Hopefully after that I'll be able to find the mayor and talk to him," Parker said and we drove off.

We found the mayor's wife and kids in her family plot. This was a beautiful spot at the back of the cemetery by a pond which is fed by a creek. "Come on," Parker said and led the way.

"Mr. and Mrs. Carlisle I'm very sorry for your loss. But I'm here to tell you he didn't kill your daughter and grandchildren," Parker said out loud and I almost jumped off the ground when Mr. and Mrs. Carlisle appeared.

"My dear child the note was on his body," Mr. Carlisle said.

"Yes sir that's true but he didn't do this. Your daughter and grandchildren will tell you that he didn't do it," Parker said then Lillith and her four daughters appeared.

"Lillith, oh my dears. Can you come have a hug?" Mrs. Carlisle asked.

"That would be wonderful!" Lillith exclaimed and they embraced and the tears flowed. Parker and I backed up and turned around so they could be together.

"Mother, Father this young woman speaks the truth Milo did not harm us, he rushed in and tried to help us but was hit on the head and rendered unconscious," Lillith said.

"Well who did it?" Mr. Carlisle asked.

"I'm not sure but it was not a man even though our murderer wanted us to think that. Even after we crossed over the true identity was hidden. The only person who knows is Milo and the killer," Lillith said and looked at Parker.

"You know who did it don't you?" Lillith asked.

"I'm almost positive but I'd like to ask your husband. Is there a personal item of his hidden away that I may touch?" Parker asked.

"Yes there is. Go to the cave that you can only hear but not see in the green meadow below the orchard. There inside the cave you'll find a ledge and on that ledge you will find what you seek. Now I must take my children home. Mother, Father would you like to come home with us?" Lillith asked.

"Oh my dear, we would love that!" Mr. and Mrs. Carlisle exclaimed in unison and they disappeared.

"Parker how do you do that?" I asked in awe of my very best friend.

"I don't know I just can and do. Come on let's go find the cave. Can I drive?" Parker asked.

"Yeah you know where it's at don't you?" I asked.

"Yeah. It's on the other side of Popsville, up a dirt road that looks like it's a dead end. Where the dirt road ends we'll walk about two miles to the orchard; through it to the meadow and then we'll find the cave," Parker said and off we went.

CHAPTER FOUR
TROUBLED TIMES BEGIN

We left the cemetery and went back to Annie's Diner. "Parker what are we doin'? We just ate," I said.

"I know, but when I make contact I get very hungry and since I've got to contact the mayor, I want to eat something else. Then I'll eat something else after I talk to the mayor. I don't know why I don't weigh eight hundred pounds," Parker said and laughed.

"Because you've got the metabolism of a humming bird. It also doesn't hurt because you're so tall," I said and tried not to laugh too hard.

Once again we were on the road and Parker was driving. We found the road we needed and drove to the end and parked. I looked out the window and saw the first obstacle, a fence. "Oh god," I groaned.

Parker looked out the window and smiled. "Marsh it won't be bad. Look at the ditch see how the fence stretches over it, you'll be able to walk right under it," Parker said, put her hand over her mouth and tried very hard not to laugh but it didn't work.

I just looked at her. The last time we had to navigate a fence we were doing something we weren't supposed to do at my insistence and I got stuck on it. I ripped my jacket; I might add it was my new jacket and my shirt to shreds. I cut my hand and if that wasn't bad enough I had to get a tetanus shot! I didn't think this little adventure could get any worse but it did. I got such a bad cold; I missed a week of school!

I just looked at Parker and grunted, "Well we'll see."

We made it under the fence without a hitch. I was able to sail right under it because of the depth of the ditch. Parker on the other hand had to hunker down but she made it without anything happening. We made our way to the orchard and came out on the other side. "This is beautiful!" I gushed looking at the beautiful green of the clearing before us.

We climbed over another fence, this one was a split rail and I managed it with ease, thank god. Once in the clearing we had no problem finding the cave. There was a rim around the meadow and on the far side water could be heard falling in an underground cavern.

We went to the spot where we could hear the water and just stood there. "How are we gonna get in there?" I asked.

Parker didn't say anything she just shrugged and squatted down. "Marsh look at that over there. See that darker spot of green. It's hangin' down from the top and it's on the ground, you see it," Parker said and pointed.

"What is that? Is it safe to walk on?" I asked.

Parker looked at me and said, "I can talk to the dead but I know nothin' about this," and we both started to laugh.

"God Parker, you're something else. Well let's go check it out," I said.

We skirted around the edge of the rim, the closer we got to the darker green we could see that it was ivy. It looked as if there might be something behind the ivy drape. "Parker look at that. There's an opening behind the ivy," I said.

We moved the ivy aside and a large opening was revealed. I was able to walk through it but since Parker is so tall she had to duck down and she still scratched her back on the top of the opening. We found some candles and matches that were left from another explorer. Once they were lit we were able to look around. There on the opposite wall was the niche and in this niche was a box. "Parker look!" I exclaimed.

"Marsh this is it. I should be able to get the information we need," Parker said as she picked up the box and opened it.

Inside the box was a pair of cuff links, a pocket watch and a wallet. Parker picked these up, smiled and then started to laugh. "Oh Mayor Hornbark you're something. He knows who killed them but he's not gonna tell me here. We have to go to his grave."

Before Parker could say another word, I just butted right in. "Parker I've got some questions, who put this box here? How are we gonna find his grave."

"Marsh I was just about to tell you where he's at," Parker said.

"Oops sorry, go on please," I said bowed and giggled.

"His wife did. They would often go on scavenger hunts. These were put here just a couple of days before all hell was set loose upon his family. The person who killed his family followed and cut him down. They drug him all the way to the east side of the orchard and buried him at the base of a large boulder. His resting place is on the edge of the church yard. He was placed there because no one would have ever thought to look for him so close to town," Parker said.

"Parker I've been there several times; do you know how many boulders there are? How far is that from here?" I asked.

"I know there are several large rocks and boulders. But this is the one that's shaped like a mushroom. It's two or three miles from here so we may as well get goin'," Parker said and we started to the car.

"I was hopin' we'd go this way," I said with relief. I figured since we're going to the car, it must be pretty important. If it wouldn't have been Parker would have walked there and back, of course I would have followed her.

We drove back the way we came, drove passed the cemetery and turned left up a small one lane road that borders the cemetery. We parked at the end of the lane in the parking lot that is set up for anyone who wants to walk the orchard, cemetery and visit the church.

We walked through the cemetery, skirted the edge of the orchard and there sat the boulder. We started walking around the base when Parker just stopped and I ran into her, "Sorry about that," I said.

"Don't worry about it. Hello Mr. Mayor, how are you today?" Parker said out loud and the form of Mayor Milo Hornbark slowly started to appear.

"I'm doing just fine. What brings you two young ladies here?" the mayor asked.

"Please excuse me for not introducing ourselves. This is Marsha Larkwood and my name is Parker MacStuart. Well, what brings us here is a very painful question which I must ask and hopefully you can supply us with the answer," Parker said.

"Well it's very nice to meet both of you, please call me Milo. Ask your question even though I'm sure I know what it is," Milo said.

Parker sighed a great sigh and then asked, "Milo could you tell us who took the lives of your wife and children?" and we waited for the answer.

"I hate to tell, I'd rather let sleeping dogs lie, it's in the past and knowing the answer won't help my family or bring them back," Milo said and the tears were streaming down his face.

"Milo that's where you're wrong. The answer could very well save the lives of many people. The answer could also bring you closer to your family," Parker said hotly and just glared at him. Dead or alive when Parker gives a person that look they wilt before her and then do or tell her what she needs to hear.

"How can the murderer be of any harm to anyone, they have long since left this life?" Milo asked.

"Because I feel their strength, they're very strong. In life they practiced the black arts and have only grown in strength. Something that was very precious to them in life has been found. If they aren't stopped and their hatred is released upon the living many more innocents will die just like your family that you love and long for," Parker said.

Milo slumped to the ground and slammed his fist down on the hard dried earth making an indentation in it. "Damn her, damn her! She held me in a spell! Damn her black soul! Gracie Mannion took the lives of my family from me because my grief was so extreme I took my own life. I pinned the note to my chest proclaiming to the world who killed my family, but she found me first!" Milo cried out in agony and started sobbing.

"Milo, my dearest husband," Lillith said as she appeared with her daughters.

Milo jumped up and clapped his hands over his mouth. Lillith, girls," came his muffled cry.

"Milo I knew you would never do anything like that unless you were under a spell. It would never have been broken had I not gotten that letter," Lillith said.

"Letter, what letter? Who sent it? I owe them many thanks for breaking the spell but the cost," and Milo fell silent.

"Milo, my dearest, it's all in the past. I know the truth so do the girls. I don't know who sent the note but I'm glad they did. Parker were all your questions answered?" Lillith asked.

"Yes ma'am they were. I hope and pray you have nothin' but happiness from this moment forward," Parker said.

"Thank you my dear and I do not think that will be a problem. Milo are you coming?" Lillith asked and held her hand out to Milo.

Milo grabbed her hand and turned to Parker, "Thank you for everything. I hope everything turns out for the best. Come my family," they walked off then vanished.

"Parker do you know who wrote the note?" I asked.

"Rosy Whipnickly. She saw what was happening and didn't like it. She tried to warn Milo's wife in person on more than one occasion but she paid her no heed. So she tried to write her but Gracie found them. When Rosy left town and arrived at her new home she mailed the letter that Milo's wife received," Parker said.

"Parker how could my aunt do something like that. Well Grandfather did say something about her goin' crazy and several people were killed. What is goin' on?" I asked.

"The reason she killed was to eliminate her competition. Gracie thought with Milo's family gone she'd have him all to herself. Why she did it the way she did I don't know so I need to talk to your grandfather some more. There are some missing pieces to the puzzle. I'm almost certain that what's goin' on is because something precious to her has been disturbed. All we have to do is figure out what it is," Parker said.

"What do we do now?" I asked.

"We're goin' back to my house. You're not goin' anywhere near your house. You'll have to wear my stuff until I get your things," Parker said.

"It must be bad if you want me to wear your clothes. You know they're just a little big on me," I said and giggled.

"Oh brother," Parker said and giggled. Once she was composed she continued, "Yes it is, your aunt wants you. I'm not exactly sure why, that's why we're goin' straight to my house," and that was the end of that discussion.

We went straight to Parker's house and were met at the door by her mother. "Mom, Marsh has to stay with us for the next couples of weeks. She can't go home for anything or under any circumstances," Parker said very seriously.

"Okay Parker that's not a problem. It's been far too long for a good visit. Marsha you're more than welcome and can stay for as long as possible," Momma Cora said and hugged me to her.

"Well come along then. Marsha you know where your room is and don't worry about anything. We'll make sure you're as snug as a bug in a rug. Why don't you go on up and freshen up a bit. I need to borrow Parker for a few minutes," Momma Cora said and kissed my forehead.

Once I was out of sight Mom turned to me and said, "Tell me what's goin' on. That poor girl looks terrible."

"Mom do you remember the story about Mayor Milo Hornbark and his family?"

"Yeah I do. What's that got to do with Marsha?" Mom asked.

"Marsh's Aunt Gracie killed Milo's family. When Milo killed himself Gracie found his body before anyone else did, she was also the one that destroyed the note. Now for some reason Gracie wants Marsh, I really think Gracie wants to take Marsh's body and Marsh will be no more. Mom I don't think she's strong enough to fight her, that's why I brought her here," I said.

"Oh god! Parker what do you want me to do?" Mom asked.

"I need you to keep her here, I don't care if she comes up with a story, she can't leave here. I'm goin' back to her house to get her some clothes and see what I can find. Mom please be careful," I said.

"Parker I will. I won't let anyone in or Marsha out. Baby you're not in danger are you?" Mom asked with great concern and rubbed my cheek.

"No I'm not; the only one in danger is Marsh. Now I've got to get goin'. I'll be back as soon as I can," I said, gave her a kiss and took off.

I got to Marsh's house, I went to unlock the door and it opened up on its own. "Welcome Parker," Mr. Larkwood said as he beckoned me into the house.

"Thank you Mr. Larkwood. I'm glad you're here. I need to talk to you about Gracie," I said.

"Parker please come with me. I have something to show you," Mr. Larkwood said and led me to the basement.

"Parker over there on that wall there's an opening would you get what I hid in there out of it please. Try as I might I just can't seem to do it," Mr. Larkwood said.

"Sure I'll do it for you. The reason you can't get to it is because you haven't been over on the other side that long," I said and walked to the spot. I squatted down, pulled off the cover, peeked in and then stuck my hand in the opening and felt around. Just as I was about to give up, my fingers brushed against something.

"I got it!" I exclaimed and pulled it out.

"Open it child, open it!" Mr. Larkwood exclaimed.

I pulled the box open and found a letter. "This is the only thing in the box," I said and handed Mr. Larkwood the letter completely forgetting he couldn't hold on to it.

Mr. Larkwood reached for the letter but his fingers went through it and it fluttered to the floor. "Oh dear god the books are gone! The books are gone!" he moaned.

"What books?" I asked.

"Two diaries; one from Rosy Whipnickly and one from Gracie. There was a story that come down through the family about these books. It was said that the diary of Rosy Whipnickly was what pushed Gracie over the edge. You see she was always a little off," and he sighed a great sigh.

"Gracie always thought people were out to get her that everybody was against her and that everybody hated her. None of it was true, my mother used to tell stories that had been passed down through the family about how good Gracie was and how people would respond to her with kindness. The story goes that just before Gracie's husband died; she took a great interest in the black arts and voodoo hoping this would cure him. Once her husband died, Gracie gave up her children; she had to they found her to be unfit to raise them. After that she threw herself into her new "religion" and she lost her soul to evil. Several people around town claimed they fell under Gracie's spell; they were all men with means, one of them happened to be the mayor. As soon as she set her sights on him, well the man didn't stand a chance."

"So when Rosy left, Gracie was heartbroken but she felt better when she read the diary that was somehow left behind. That diary became almost a bible to her and according to the story it spoke to her then it possessed her. So much in fact that she'd take on the personality of the writer, meaning Rosy."

"Then strange things started to happen. People would disappear and months later their mutilated corpses would be found. This went on for several years and would have went on for several more had it not been for a detective named Roy Marshall."

"He had found the latest victim and heard about the others. He studied them for several months looking for a connection between all of them. The only one he could find was Gracie."

"He went to confront Gracie with this information, she denied it of course, but the detective just kept at her and she snapped. She excused herself and went into the kitchen on the pretense of getting some coffee for them. When she returned it wasn't Gracie and she attacked the detective with a butcher knife."

"The only thing that saved him was his size; he also had two others with him who rushed in to see the attack. They subdued her all the while she was ranting going from our tongue to that of a British woman."

"There wasn't a trial; she was put into an asylum, the very best of the day once there she received the greatest care. The doctors at the asylum thought Gracie was making great progress, so great in fact they gave her many special privileges. But that all changed when she managed to get her hands on a knife and butchered two of the staff. Her privileges were suspended, she was put back in her room, her top notch care continued; the best of the day and she spent the rest of her very long, tortured life in the care of the doctors," Mr. Larkwood said and fell silent.

"How come she's after Marsh?" I asked.

"Because Parker, you and I both know she's impressionable. Those books have to be found!"

I came downstairs to find Parker but she seemed to have disappeared. "Momma Cora where's Parker?"

"She said she had some errands to run. I'm sure she's gone to get your clothes. Marsha are you feelin' alright, you look a little tired. Why don't you go lay down? I'll send Parker up when she gets home. Now go to bed and I'll bring you something to eat a little later."

"Okay, I am kinda tired. You don't mind do you?" I asked.

"Not at all dear. Now you go to bed," Momma Cora said and kissed me on the forehead.

I went upstairs and laid down but I couldn't get to sleep. I felt as if something was pulling me to my bag. I walked over to it and opened it up, to my surprise there were the two diaries I had put in the desk drawer. How in the heck did they get here?

The first diary flipped open and the name Gracie Mannion stared up at me and hypnotized me. I was compelled to turn the page and there were the words Trevor is cheating you.

"I knew it! I knew it! I'm gonna look up my items or those similar and check their prices!" I declared and slammed the book shut.

Sure enough I found my items on the internet and sure enough he had cheated me. As I put my laptop up I vowed my revenge upon Trevor, but I didn't know how. The answer was revealed to me on the third page of the diary.

I would be seeing Trevor next weekend and he was going to get a great surprise! But first I had to give Parker the slip, I don't have a clue how I'll do that, but something will turn up.

CHAPTER FIVE
HIDDEN BOOKS

I heard the rap on the door and went into a panic; I had to hide the diaries. "Just a minute, I'll be right there!" I called out and turned around to find that they were gone.

I opened the door and there stood Parker, good lord she's an imposing character. "Parker I'm sorry, I was in the bathroom. Thanks for bringin' this stuff for me. I truly do appreciate it," I said, I truly did appreciate it, I just wasn't paying lip service to her.

"I hope I brought you enough," Parker said and paused. I know she had some questions and knowing her as I do she'll just be blunt with her question.

"Marsh where'd you put the books from the basement?" Parker asked.

I just stared at her; this wasn't what I thought she would ask me. "Sorry, that question took me by surprise. I put them in the top left desk drawer in the library. I didn't read them. Why do you ask?"

"Your grandfather had me look for them. I found the box with the letter in it. Why did you put the empty box back in the basement?" Parker asked.

"Parker I didn't put the box back there, I put it all in the desk drawer. Who did that," and I fell silent and then a thought came to me, "My god it was Trevor! That cheat put them there. It has to be him," I said.

"Marsh why would Trevor do that?" Parker asked.

"Because he's that way. Can we just forget it? This is just very stressful for me. Please Parker," I cried and latched on to her.

Parker hugged me back, "Okay Marsh. I'll drop it; I'll worry about it later. You want something to eat or drink?" Parker asked.

"No, I'm just worn out. I want to go take a nap," I replied.

"Sure, go to bed and I'll check on you later," Parker said and left the room.

I had every intention of going to sleep but the books appeared and opened. The first page that was shown to me was the end of the diary. "I have no regrets for the things I have done. I have avenged my beloved mother and sisters, may their saintly souls rest in heaven. May my father, piece of gutter trash that he is, rot in the fiery bowels of Hell for all eternity."

I started thumbing through Rosy's diary and I thought I was going to vomit. It went into great and gory detail of how she killed the women. It listed all the well-known Ripper victims and several that weren't published or weren't connected to the Ripper. She had also collected every piece of paper concerning the murders. She wrote and wrote and wrote, letting all her hatred for her father flow from her and into her journal. This was her therapy.

I closed Rosy's diary and opened up Gracie's. It started off with her meeting Rosy right after her husband died. It seemed it was a fast friendship from the get-go, actually it sounded as if Gracie's relationship bordered on obsession.

"Boy this is depressing," I said to the room.

There wasn't much going on in the diary, Gracie seemed very stable until Rosy left. When that happened she seemed to have lost something and it became very strange.

"Today was a very sad one for me. My very best friend, my sister, my soul mate left me today. She said she had to follow her heart and mine is broken."

"My god she was obsessed with her," I said.

"Who was obsessed with whom? I thought you left those home?" Parker asked and I about jumped off the bed.

"I did, but when I came in here they were here! Honest to god Parker I didn't bring them here! You've got to believe me!" I cried.

"Marsh I believe you and now I know why you said those things about Trevor. Marsh you've got to get rid of these things, especially the one from Gracie," Parker said and grabbed it so fast I couldn't react.

The gas fireplace roared to life and Parker threw Gracie's diary on the fire. She had to restrain me from jumping in after it. "Stop it Marsha! That book is evil! If it's not destroyed you will be lost. Now we stand a chance!" Parker yelled.

"Gracie go home, go to the light! You're dead, now go home to your family! You leave Marsha alone! Do you understand me! Go home now!" Parker yelled and held on to me.

Gracie appeared and she was none too happy. "How dare you tell me what to do! Do you know who I am and what I did?" she asked.

"Yeah I know who you are you're a coward and a butcher. **Because you didn't get what you wanted you killed innocent children and an innocent lady. You brought shame to your family! That's who you are! Now leave!**" Parker bellowed.

This stopped Gracie in her tracks, Parker was livid and a livid Parker is scary. I've seen her angry but I've never seen her this angry, she even scared me. Then I noticed why Gracie stopped, there was a white glow pulsing off Parker and it surrounded us. The glow looked to have substance to it, it seemed thick and I felt safe inside it standing with Parker, holding onto her. Plus I could hear static electricity snapping, popping and sparking all around the glow and a foot around it.

"I tell you again to leave on your own accord. If you don't you will be forcibly removed," Parker said as four men in white tunics with red crosses on them appeared.

"I will not go and you cannot make me," Gracie sneered defiantly.

"So be it," Parker said and she nodded her head.

The four men surrounded her; a great light blazed and they were gone. "Parker is she gone for good?" I asked.

"I sure as god hope so. When these guys take a person its bad news. Marsh would you be willin' to give me Rosy's diary?" Parker asked.

"Sure," I said. I snatched it off the bed as if it was on fire. I handed it to Parker and a weight had been lifted off my shoulder.

"What are you gonna do with that?" I asked.

"Put it where no one will be able to get at it," Parker replied.

Just then Momma Cora burst in, eyes wide, ready to do battle; I can see where Parker gets it from. "Are you two alright? What was all the yelling about?"

"Mom we're okay. Gracie was here, now she's been taken away. Mom could you stay with marsh until I get back? I have something to do," Parker said.

"Yes Parker I can, that won't be a problem," Momma Cora said.

"Thanks Mom," Parker said and left the room.

Parker was gone for over two hours. When she came back the first words out of her mouth were, "I'm starving, let's eat," and with these words I knew she had taken care of it. I only hope that it's not too late.

"Parker will everything be alright?" I asked as I followed her downstairs to the kitchen.

"Well that depends on how strong you can be. Gracie doesn't like to lose, so she'll be gunnin' for us for the next few months maybe up to six months. During that time you'll have to be extremely careful about what you're thinking. Guard your thoughts. If you get jealous, envious or think you're bein' wronged these negative thoughts can and will feed Gracie."

"But that shouldn't be a problem because you'll be with us and I won't take no for an answer," Parker said. I looked up at her, she meant business and I swallowed hard. Her eyes are usually bright, shiny and friendly but when she gets this look on her face, they get cold and she flares her nostrils. Well when that happens it's best not to argue with her, you won't win.

"Alright Parker, I'll stay and I'll do my very best to keep all negative and hurtful thoughts away. I know if I need help you'll be there to help me. Thank you for always bein' there for me," I said, hugged her and started crying.

"You're welcome Marsh, you were there for me when I needed to talk about Penelope. This is what sisters do and we are sisters, through thick and thin we'll be there for each other," Parker said, she squeezed me so hard I thought she would break my ribs.

"Alright you two sit down and eat," Momma Cora said and ran to get the phone.

She came back into the kitchen as white as a sheet and shaking. She had tears streaming down her face. Parker jumped up knocking over her chair and rushed to her side. "Mom what's the matter?"

"That was Addie! Momma is dead! She was in London on business and some bloody fool ran her over! The funeral is Wednesday. I've got to call Will and the quads. Parker you and Marsha get packed and Parker will you call and make the reservations. If we can get out tonight, that would be perfect if not make them for tomorrow," Momma Cora said and off she went.

"Parker I'm so sorry, I'm so sorry," I said and started to cry.

"Thanks Marsh. As soon as I get the reservations made we'll go to your place and you can get your clothes," Parker said and sniffed.

"Is it safe for me to go home? Are you sure you're okay?" I asked.

"Yeah it's safe because we'll only be there for a little bit and yeah I'm okay as I can be. I got to talk to her last week, we got to say I love you to each other, we were at peace and neither one of us had any regrets," Parker said and out the door we went.

When we got back Father Will, that's what I've always called Parker's father, Wills, Grant, Davey and Dom the quads were all home, they were packed and waiting for us so we could leave. "Come on ladies get a move on, we've got to go! Parker put us on standby and we've got seats now! So let's get goin'!" Father Will exclaimed and hustled us out the door.

Father Will drove like a mad man to get us to the airport on time. I was scared to death; all I could see was the accident that took my family from me. I don't know why we didn't get pulled over by the police for speeding or how we survived our trip to the airport! Good god he was weaving in and out of traffic in that huge van of theirs as if it was a sports car!

I was so glad when we got to the airport in one piece I wanted to get down and kiss the ground! Parker had to grab me because I was getting down on my knees to give thanks, "Marsh don't you're fine. You are a little green around the gills, but you never had anything to worry about. Dad is a great driver and fancies himself a race car driver," Parker said and giggled.

We checked in and just made it with five minutes to spare. The takeoff went without a hitch and soon I settled down next to Parker, my very best friend who I considered my sister. "Well that went well. What adventures do you think we'll have in the future?" I asked.

"I don't know only time will tell," Parker said and squeezed my arm.

We landed and were met by Parker's aunt and uncle. Once all the luggage was loaded up we went straight to Briargate. "Jonathan and Arlene are already at Briargate," Addie said and I thought Parker was going to blow a gasket.

"Not a word Parker, not a word. We all know how you feel, we've heard it on more than one occasion," Father Will said.

All eyes seemed to be on Parker. "I won't say anything," Parker said.

She then turned to me and whispered, "This is gonna be fun. Jonathan and Arlene are a bit greedy. I'm sure they're already makin' lists of what they think is rightfully theirs. I can't tell you how glad I'll be when this is all over."

"Is it gonna be that bad?" I asked.

"Yeah it will. Well Marsh the fun starts now," Parker said and we entered the melee.

We walked in and I was shocked at the number of people inside the house. Some of them were visibly upset, as soon as they saw us they rushed to us. "Parker how many kids did your Grandmother have?" I asked.

"Well let's see. There's mom, Addie, Jonathan, Mitchell, Thomas, Marjorie, Francis, Elizabeth, Mary, Robert, James, Henry, Laura and Margaret," Parker said.

"Good lord," I said.

"She had a large brood and some of them are very nice, decent people while others are greedy, uncaring slugs. Crud! I hate some of these people. Some of them are nothin' more than bloodsuckers. I just hope they get absolutely nothin'; they deserve nothin'. Dirty blood suckers," Parker mumbled.

Parker looked over at her mother and she nodded. "Come on Marsh, let's go find Gerald. He's the butler and a very good guy. To me he is more family to Grandmother than some of her flesh and blood, they were very close. Sarah is his wife and she's a wonderful woman," Parker said as we made our way toward the kitchen.

"Miss Parker, it is good to see you again. I am heartily sorry for your loss," Mr. Cosgrove said.

"Please call me Parker and thank you very much. You have my condolences; I know you and Mrs. Cosgrove were very fond of Grandmother. Thank you for takin' such good care of her. And I'm so glad to see you again," Parker said.

"Yes Miss; Sarah and I were very fond of her. She was a grand lady," Mr. Cosgrove said and wiped away a tear. Parker couldn't help herself and she reached out and hugged him.

"I'm sorry miss," Mr. Cosgrove said and he sniffed again. Parker finally let go of him but grabbed his hand as if he were going to run away.

"Mr. Cosgrove this is my very best friend Marsha Larkwood and yes she was a grand lady," Parker said.

"Good to meet you miss," Mr. Cosgrove said and Parker finally let go of his hand so he could shake mine.

"Nice to meet you also," I replied.

"Now miss, I mean Parker, what can I do for you?" Mr. Cosgrove asked.

"Mom wanted me to ask you where our rooms were at. She wants to get away from you know who," Parker said.

Mr. Cosgrove smiled, "Oh yes miss I know who you mean. Miss you and your family have the same rooms you had when you were last here," and a cloud passed his face.

He was going to say something else but Parker stopped him. "You don't have to watch what you say to or around me. You don't have to apologize to me for anything you've been nothin' but kind to me and I appreciate it more than you'll ever know," Parker said and hugged him again.

"Now if you'll excuse us I'm gonna tell Mom and then Marsh and I are gonna our room. I'm sure not in the mood for some of them. Feelin' like I do I'm afraid I just might have to say something and it wouldn't be pleasant," Parker said and kissed Mr. Cosgrove on the cheek and hugged him once again.

Parker made her way back to her Momma Cora and several of her aunts and a couple of her uncles. Father Will and the quads were holding their own with a knot of her uncles and a couple of aunts. Parker told Momma Cora they had the same rooms as last time. As soon as that little chore was done she led me to our room.

"Good god Parker, this place is huge! Is this all the original house?" I asked.

"No, this is the newer section built in the mid 1800's. Our rooms are in the original house built in 1445. It's my favorite part of the house. It's very homey feeling and I have a lot of friends and acquaintances here," Parker said.

"Wow! That's fascinating! Parker something has been naggin' at me and I don't want you to think I'm selfish and I'm the only one that matters, but,"

She cut me off, "Marsh don't, I understand and I know it's not about you. You have nothin' to worry about. You're safer here than any place else. There are many spirits under the roof and all of them are cordial, helpful and friendly. I've always felt safe here especially when Penelope left and found happiness," Parker said and smiled.

As we walked to our room we would stop at certain areas; several portraits, a couple of suits of armor, a table, the third step on the second set of stairs and the list went on and on. When we would stop Parker would give me a brief history of who was there, when they lived and how they died. She would also tell me if the spirits were earthbound and if they could or wanted to they would pay us a visit.

We finally got to our room, it took us over an hour but it had been a very interesting hour. Our luggage was already there and they looked so small sitting in this room. "Good grief Parker this room is huge! Well why shouldn't it be considering this house is the size of a museum! How do you navigate this place without getting lost!" I exclaimed.

"Well I do have some help," Parker said and we both started laughing.

Just then Momma Cora, and her aunts Addie, Marjorie and Francis stormed in and slammed the door. It was hard to figure out who was madder. "What is wrong with those people?" Parker's Aunt Addie asked.

"I don't even know some of them. What part of the tree did they fall out of?" Parker's Aunt Marjorie asked.

"I'm hoping the others can calm them down. But on the other hand there is no calming Jonathan and Arlene down," Parker's Aunt Francis said.

"Nobody can calm them down except Momma," Momma Cora said and sighed and then continued, "I know he's our oldest brother but I've never seen anybody as insensitive as he and Arlene! I'd like to line everyone up and slap some sense into them! You know it would serve them right and they'd deserve it; I truly hope they get nothin'. I know that sounds terrible to say of my own brothers and sisters but some of them, argh!" Momma Cora snapped.

"Mom, Aunt Addie, Aunt Marjorie, Aunt Francis, what's the matter?" Parker asked.

"They're bloody rude and ruthless. Oh not all of them but Jonathan has always been able to stir up the pot," Aunt Addie said.

"Those dirty blood suckers are taking inventory of all the items in the house and gettin' them appraised!" Momma Cora snapped.

"But why? Can't you stop them Aunt Addie?" Parker asked.

She snorted and said, "Oh bloody hell! Jonathan thinks because he's the oldest he's in charge and gets it all. I've tried talking to him but it's useless."

As if on cue Jonathan, his wife Arlene and an appraiser walked into the room. I looked at Parker and knew there was going to be trouble. I also saw Momma Cora touch Parker's arm; I can't wait for the show to start. "Excuse me didn't anyone teach you any manners? You get out now or I'll help you out," Parker said to the shocked appraiser. He left without saying a word, the fear clearly shone in his eyes.

"How dare you come into a room without knocking. I suggest you leave this room and do your appraisal elsewhere," Parker said and the storm known as Parker was turning into a tornado.

Jonathan looked at Parker, who stood over 6' 10" in her stocking feet, he gave his intrusion a thought, he didn't turn to leave but he didn't try to go any farther into the room. His greed got the better of him and he said, "This isn't your house and I can do as I please."

I guess he thought this would put Parker in her place; he obviously had no clue who he was dealing with. "Well Uncle Jonathan this isn't your house either, even if it was your house you never enter a room without knocking."

"How dare you talk to me that way. You are rude and of low birth," Jonathan said.

"Well since we are related Uncle Jonathan, the same can be said of you," Parker said and smiled. Anyone who knew Parker would have quit now. She is usually the sweetest, nicest person on the face of the earth, but push her and she won't hesitate to point out your flaws. And do it in such a way where everyone hears it.

All Jonathan could do was sputter. "You know Parker mother wasn't fond of you at all. I don't see how anyone could find you attractive because of your size, you should be a man."

"Well Uncle Jonathan at least I have a chin. How's it feel to have a weak chin and defective genes? You should also have been born a man but you weren't. You have no children and have been married forever. How do we know you're a man at all, for all we know you're a woman, god knows your small enough to be one. The only thing we know for sure is you were born a dirty, sniveling, chinless, spineless little weasel. The only reason you have a wife is because of who and what Grandmother was. Now get out of this room before I pick you up and throw you out on your butt! Oh and by the way you weren't a favorite of Grandmother either," Parker said and walked to the door. She opened it up waved Jonathan and Arlene out and they finally left the room in a huff.

"Parker," Momma Cora said. She started laughing and was joined by Parker's aunt. Soon we were all laughing so hard we were hanging on to each other.

"Well I imagine Jonathan will steer clear of you and us for a while," Aunt Addie said.

"Well come on ladies, let's go get something to eat. I'm starving!" Momma Cora said and off we went.

The next few days flew by and we were off to the church for the funeral. It really was a beautiful service, beautifully done and many tears were shed. All of them were genuine except Jonathan; he couldn't have shed a genuine tear unless it directly impacts him.

Once the funeral was done we went to the cemetery and made our way to the family plot. This service was very informal, anyone who wanted to speak could. Momma Cora and Father Will spoke, Mr. and Mrs. Freemantle, that's Parker's Aunt Addie and Uncle Henry and several others also spoke.

Jonathan got up and went on and on and on. I thought the priest was going to have to tell him to sit down and shut up. He finally wrapped it up and I had to catch myself; I almost started clapping. "Is there anyone else who'd like to say a few words?" the priest asked.

"I would," Parker said and I almost fell of my chair.

"I just wanted to tell you how much I admired my Grandmother," and Jonathan snorted.

"I truly respected her and even though we weren't very close I loved her very much," Parker said.

She was about to say something else but Jonathan butted in, "You, Parker, were not a favorite and all your words will not get you a part of the fortune."

Everybody gasped but it didn't seem to faze Parker. "You're right we weren't that close but we made peace. I have nothin' to regret. And fortune be damned, I'm here sayin' that I loved her not for any gains; I just want to share my feelings. So until we meet again on the other side, Grandmother I love and miss you," Parker said and Jonathan snorted again.

"Thank you Parker," Marjorie, Parker's Grandmother said for all to hear and she appeared before all who attended.

"You're very welcome Grandmother. Did you make it without any problems?" Parker asked.

"Yes I did dear; Penelope met me, thank you for asking. I appreciate it."

"As for you Jonathan you need to take a few lessons from this young woman. You are nothing but a greedy, uncaring man. There will be some trying times coming, some good and some bad. Cora, Will cherish this young lady, she is one of a kind."

"Parker I'm deeply sorry for not giving you the love you deserved your entire life. What I didn't give you in life, until the end I will give it to you in my afterlife. Now my lovelies I bid you peace," Grandmother said and she was gone.

The cemetery emptied as if the plague was coming in with the wind. "Wow Parker. You sure know how to clear the crowd," Momma Cora said and we all laughed.

"Addie, Henry do you want to come with Will and I, we're gonna visit Penelope," Momma Cora said.

"We'd love to," Mrs. Fremantle said and they walked off.

"Parker aren't you goin'?" I asked.

"Not yet. Mom, Dad and the quads need to talk to her by themselves. Besides that, she's over there," Parker said and pointed to the hedgerow.

"Oh my god!" I gasped.

"Hi Penelope, Sir Phillip. How are you? I'm so glad to see both of you! Have you been able to spend much time with Grandmother?" Parker asked.

"Parker come here," Penelope said and grabbed her sister.

"I'm so glad to see you, you too Marsha. I'm so glad you're here. No I haven't she's been busy. I do know that there's gonna be a huge shock when the will is read," Penelope said.

"What do you mean?" Parker asked.

"You will see Lady Parker. I have been making great progress in speaking this modern language," Sir Phillip said hugged Parker. He stepped away to let the sisters and I be alone.

We had a great visit, even though it was a short one. "Parker, my dearest sister, I've got to go. I have to see Mom, Dad, the quads, aunts, uncles and the list goes on and on," she said and they both started laughing.

"I hope you understand," Penelope said and held Parker's hand.

"Yeah I do, now go. I'll see you later," Parker said.

"Nice to have seen you Penelope," I said.

"Nice to have seen you also Marsha. Parker see you later," Penelope said and they were gone.

"Let's go back to the house. I can't wait to see what surprises the reading of the will brings," Parker said.

"Well you'll only have to wait two more days," I said and we started off to Briargate.

CHAPTER SIX
BEGINNING OF RAGE

For the next two and a half days Parker took me all around the area, she would make a fantastic tour guide. She told me things that no one else could possibly know. But because of her abilities it was if I had lived their lives.

It was now time for Parker and her family to visit the solicitor; they were the last to find out the contents of the will. Parker and I had several long talks about the contents; she hoped her parents and the quads would get something nice. She didn't care if she got anything, just so her family did. Momma Cora heard her say that and just shook her head and smiled as if she knew something Parker didn't.

I was going to stay at Briargate and get in Gerald's and Sarah's way trying to help them, well Parker had other plans. So I ended up going with Parker and her family. When we walked in and Jonathan and Arlene saw me I thought they were going to explode. "She can't be here, she's not family!" Jonathan snapped and the solicitor agreed.

"I'm sorry; I didn't think it would be a problem. We'll just go and nose around for a little bit," Parker said and we stared to leave.

"Parker, Marsha don't go very far," Momma Cora said.

"Did you say Parker?" the solicitor asked and she shook her head.

"I'm afraid you'll have to stay. Miss if you want I can have one of my staff show you around," Mr. Barlowe said.

"Well that would be very nice. Thank you very much I really appreciate it," I said.

Mr. Barlowe buzzed his assistant David and in walked one of the most handsome men I have ever seen in my life. My knees turned to mush and I thought I was going to fall. I looked over at Parker, she had this look on her face and shook her head no and she started to get up.

"Yes Mr. Barlowe," David said.

Before Mr. Barlowe could say another word Parker asked, "Mr. Barlowe would you excuse us for just a minute?"

"Well this is highly unusual but make it quick," Mr. Barlowe said.

Parker led me outside and said, "Marsh please be on your guard with this one. He's nice to look at but he's black inside. I'd feel better if you wouldn't go."

"Parker you're jealous. You don't want me to be happy do you?" I asked, shocked at her behavior.

"Marsha," Parker said and stopped," You know what, just forget it. I just don't want you to get hurt, but if you don't want to listen, so be it," and Parker started to walk off.

I grabbed her arm and said, "Hold it that's it, you're not gonna say anything else?"

"Nope. You don't want to listen so I'm done talkin'. Now let's go in and you can go off with David for your tour," Parker said, took my hand and led me back in.

"Well I'm glad you two are back. David would you be so kind as to escort Miss," and he stopped.

"Larkwood. Marsha Larkwood," I said.

"Would you be so kind and escort Miss Larkwood for about two hours and then bring her back here. Thank you very much David," Mr. Barlowe said.

"Miss Larkwood," David said and offered me his arm.

"Well thank you," I said as we left the room I turned and stuck my tongue out at Parker.

Mom turned to me and whispered, "What was that all about?"

"I told her that I didn't feel right about David and she needed to be careful. She told me that I was jealous and I didn't want her to be happy. I told her that wasn't it at all. You know Mom I love Marsh as a sister but sometimes when she gets this way I'd like to slap her," I said.

"Damn what's wrong with that girl? Will this behavior cause her harm with Gracie?" Mom asked.

"Yes it could. I've warned her several times. But when she gets this way it sure won't help her and since Gracie is out to get her this will sure as heck help her," Parker said and sighed.

As soon as Marsh left with David, Mr. Barlowe began by starting a movie and on it was Grandmother. "If you are watching this then I am no longer of this earth. I am not going to tell you I am of sound mind and body because you all know that I am. If you have any questions regarding my state of mind take it up with Mr. Barlowe, but know this, if any of you contest the will you get nothing and my entire estate will be put on the open market."

"She can't do that!" Jonathan yelled and jumped up.

"Jonathan please take your seat. She has every right to do it. I would advise you to be very careful with what you say and do in the next couple of hours," Mr. Barlowe warned.

"Jonathan now that your outburst is over and you've once again shown what kind of man you are I know my decision is the correct one," Grandmother said.

"Before I tell you what I have left you I have instructed Mr. Barlowe that if you throw a tantrum your inheritance will go to Addie and Henry. To you Jonathan I leave you the property in Greece, the vineyards and the property in Portugal. I also leave you a sum of money that will keep you in comfort for the rest of your lives. I want you to make these properties work and bring them back to their former glory. I know you can do this, this is your strength. I also know you were your happiest and most fulfilled at these places. Now my dear Jonathan, please be happy and at peace," Grandmother said and the movie stopped.

I was waiting for the outburst but I was shocked. Jonathan was crying, so was Arlene. "Mother, you have made this man so very happy, thank you so very much," Arlene said.

"Thank you Mummy, from the bottom of my heart. Thank you also Mr. Barlow," Jonathan said.

"You are very welcome. On your way out stop at Elizabeth's desk, she'll have papers for you to sign and will give you all the necessary paperwork and your keys. Good luck to both of you," Mr. Barlowe said and shook their hands. Once out the door the movie started again.

"Miss Larkwood where would you like to go?" David asked.

"Please call me Marsha. I don't know, I've never been here before, so lead on," I said.

"Well then let's get a quick bite to eat and then we'll do some exploring," David said.

"Sounds like a very good plan to me," I said and he offered me his arm once again.

We went to a very nice, quaint spot and had a simple but delicious lunch. The conversation was absolutely fabulous, but there was one thing a little off about him. I was beginning to think I should have listened to Parker. He was sitting so close to me as if we were lovers sharing an intimate conversation. I know I should say something but I held my tongue.

When we left the restaurant I excused myself to use the bathroom and when I came out David was on the phone. I didn't think anything about it; I just assumed it was Mr. Barlowe. "So alright then let's get the tour started," David said and grabbed my hand.

We walked around the block and a panel van pulled up next to us. The door slid open and I was pushed and pulled inside. "She's right lovely Davey, we'll clean er' up when we're done with er'," one of the men in the van laughed and we sped away.

"Let me go, what's goin' on? Let me out of here!" I screamed.

"Oh now miss, we'll pay you well enough," one of the men said.

"Oh well I don't think that will happen today," I said just waiting to make my move.

We stopped at a light and they never saw the attack coming. I grabbed the driver by the hair and smashed his face off the steering wheel. As he was screaming with pain and shock I was able to put the van in park. His friend attempted to help the driver but I kicked him in the throat. I grabbed the driver and his friend by the hair of the head and pulled them from the van into the middle of the street. Thank god for Parker and her self-defense lessons.

I was livid! I was yelling at these two stupid idiots at the top of my lungs in the middle of the street! Finally the police came, "Miss what's the matter?"

"These two jerks pulled me into that van and were gonna take me to who knows where to do who knows what to me! They have a friend named David who works for Mr. Barlowe!" I yelled and the tears were streaming down my face.

They took the two men away and drove me back to the office; we actually got there before David. The color drained from his face. "You dirty bastard!" I hissed and slapped him across the face so hard his lip was bleeding.

"How, how, how did you get away?" David asked.

"You picked the wrong girl to mess with!" I hissed and spit on him.

We went back to the police station and as David walked by us I spit on him again. I pressed charges against them all, gave the police my information and somehow got the names and addresses of my kidnappers. When that was all done Det. Smyth took me back to Mr. Barlowe's office and sat with me until the reading of the will was done.

"Miss Larkwood where did you learn those moves?" he asked.

"My very best friend, Parker and if she would have been there and did what I did, well they would be dead," I replied.

"Really, why?" Det. Smythe asked.

"Well she's extremely strong and very tall. Plus I've seen her defend herself," I said.

We waited ten more minutes and Mr. Barlowe came out of the office. "Marsh what's wrong?" Parker asked and rushed to my side.

"Miss Larkwood I see what you mean," Det. Smyth said as Parker stood next to me. She shot him a look that said you better make sure the guys who did this are severely punished or I will.

"Where is David? Did he do something to you?" Mr. Barlowe asked.

"Mr. Barlowe may I speak to you in private regarding this matter?" Det. Smyth asked.

"Yes; please come this way, we can speak in private in my office," Mr. Barlowe said.

Before Det. Smythe left he said, "Miss Larkwood you may go home. We have your information and if we need anything else we'll contact you."

"Thank you Det. Smythe, I appreciate it," I said and in they went.

"Alright Marsh what in the heck happened?" Parker demanded.

"Well I don't know what was goin' on. David kept offering his arm and grabbed my hand. I should have said something but I thought he was just being polite. Well after lunch I went to the bathroom and when I came out he was on the phone. I didn't give it a thought."

"After the phone call we went outside and started walkin'. That's when the van pulled up next to us. The door slid open so quietly I didn't even hear it. David pushed me and as I stumbled toward the van, the ones inside grabbed me and they took off."

"Well they said they'd clean me up for David and I knew I was in a lot of trouble. So I smashed the driver's face off the steering wheel and kicked the other one in the throat. I put the van in park and drug those two slimy sacks of crap out of the van by the hair and then the cops came. Parker I'm so sorry I didn't listen to you. I'm so sorry I said you were jealous. Please forgive me," I said and started to cry.

Parker hugged me and said, "Marsh don't worry about it. I forgive you even though you've done nothin' wrong."

"Thank you Parker, thank you," I sobbed. This was one very forgiving woman. She never said I told you so and she's had plenty of chances over the years to say it.

I was soon bundled up by Momma Cora and her sister Addie. "Now my dear Marsha you have nothin' to worry about. Come on let's get you home," Momma Cora said and led me to the van. We set off for Briargate and the events of the day would haunt my dreams.

CHAPTER SEVEN
VENGEANCE

Parker held me all the way to Briargate; cradling me as if I were a small child. She was singing a beautiful song about a woman who found her true love, I wonder if it's about Penelope. As I sat there listening to this beautiful song I hadn't realized how upset I was. I cried all the way there and the more I tried to pull myself together the more Parker's warning came back to me, so I cried even harder.

"It's okay Marsh, you're safe now. They won't be able to hurt you ever again. I'll tell you what if I see those lousy duck suckers my face will be the last thing they see. So now you just try to relax and go to sleep," Parker said.

"Parker am I gonna be alright, you know safe?" I asked.

"Yeah you're gonna be fine," Parker replied and I closed my eyes.

"Parker is she gonna be alright?" Mom asked.

Before I could answer Dom butted right in. "I've been appointed to ask the question. What is a duck sucker?"

"I don't know, it just popped in my head and out of my mouth," I said and the quads got a look from Dad that said to keep a civil tongue in their heads.

"Now answer the other question," Dad said.

"I don't know. If she doesn't pull herself together and put this behind her and clear her thoughts, Gracie could very well get her foot in the door. Every time this happens Gracie will see it just as if she was opening a door. The bright lights behind the open door will shine brightly inviting Gracie in. We definitely don't want this to happen. It could have dire consequences," I said.

"Marsh come on we're home. Wake up," Parker said gently as she gently woke me up.

"Thanks Parker," I said groggily.

"Come on I'll take you up to our room, you can take a bath and then take a nap," Parker said.

"Parker thanks so very much for everything," I said.

"Marsh you're more than welcome. Now you go take a long soak, I'll be downstairs gettin' you something to eat," Parker said and I went into the bathroom.

I sat in the tub for almost two hours. Even though I wasn't raped, I felt dirty and no amount of scrubbing could remove it. The longer I sat there the madder I became. My thoughts were only of getting even and causing them pain.

I thought I felt something in the room with me and that scared me. All my thoughts of vengeance went out the window and the feeling of being watched left. "Dear god help me!" I cried.

I finally started feeling better. I wasn't hurt and I was back with people who truly cared for me. So I stopped feeling sorry for myself and got out of the tub, got dressed and went downstairs. When I got down there, it was a madhouse.

"What's the matter?" I asked.

"Oh you're not gonna believe this. They let all three of them go," Father Will said.

"Why?" I asked.

"Because David has power and influence behind him," Mrs. Freemantle said.

"So they're gonna be able to do this to someone else? Figures just figures. Is there anything we can do?" I asked.

"No. Until the trial they're out. They will be followed so they won't be able to get away with anything like this again," Mr. Freemantle said.

"Well that makes me feel somewhat better. But to change the subject, how did the meeting go, I know you can't tell me I was just praying it went well," I said.

"It went very well and I would tell you if we were allowed to, even Jonathan was happy," Momma Cora said.

"I certainly understand it was the same with me. But can you tell me who got Briargate?" I asked.

"I did," Parker said and continued, "Gerald and Sarah will stay here and have a monthly allowance of fifty thousand each. I also have to go to London to take care of some business on Monday and of course Marsh you're comin' with me."

"I got several properties that I'll have to check out, figure out what I want to do with them. They're kind of spread out so there will be a lot of traveling," Parker said.

"Wow! Sounds like you're gonna be busy," I said.

"What do you mean I, it's we're gonna be busy. I figure we can take classes via the internet," Parker said.

"Oh you twisted my arm!" and we all started to laugh.

We stayed until Saturday and once again left for London. Mr. and Mrs. Freemantle were leaving on Sunday morning as were Parker's parents and brothers. After everyone was gone, it was so very quiet. I thought Parker and I were going to go nuts. "Marsh do you want to go for a ride? Maybe we can find someplace that sells ice cream," Parker said.

"Yeah let's go. Parker you'll be fine, just fine. I know you miss your family, I understand how you feel," I said.

"Thanks Marsh. I'll be okay; it will just take a couple of days. Once we're busy, it will be just fine," Parker said and smiled.

We went for our drive and we finally found an ice cream shop. We walked in, placed our order and Parker had to go back out and roll the windows up the rest of the way because it started to rain. While Parker was out David and the other two men walked in.

They saw me before I saw them. "Well, well, well, look who's here. Are you glad to see us?" David asked.

I sucked in a breath of air and tried to get out of there. "Leave me alone!" I yelled and everybody looked at me.

"She's just a little high. She'll be fine after she gets some fresh air," David said and they actually tried to pull me out of the store.

"I'd let go of her if you know what's good for you," Parker said. There was a chill in the room that was terrible, mothers grabbed their kids and left the shop, many of them on cell phones calling the police and taking pictures of this huge woman.

"Oh and who's going to make me," David sneered and turned around only to look into Parker's huge chest.

Parker was not in a good frame of mind. As much as I would like to see her kill these scum bags, I really don't want her to get into trouble. She made a V with her index and middle fingers. She slid her fingers beneath his chin until his neck touched the notch between her fingers. She then picked him up where he could look into her eyes; his feet were dangling off the floor. I guess what he saw in her eyes terrified him so badly that he wet his pants.

"Little man not on this day or any other. You're not gonna take my very best friend, my sister and rape her like you tried to last week. And if you two want to get out of here in one piece I'd sit down," Parker hissed.

They didn't want to sit down, so Parker grabbed both of them by the front of their shirts with her huge free hand and picked them up. "Are you boys comfy?" Parker asked sweetly.

"No we're not, put us down you dirty bitch!" one of them yelled then Sir Phillip arrived and everyone that was still in the ice cream shop rushed to get out.

"Didn't your parents teach you any manners?" Sir Phillip asked and smacked them on the back of their heads, then the police arrived and Sir Phillip simply vanished causing those that were looking at the unfolding events from the safety of the sidewalk to gasp and back up.

"Lady Parker is that you? Look Sam it's Lady Parker," the officer said.

"Constable Clark, Constable Weaver it's good to see you. How are you and your families doin'?" Parker asked still holding the men.

"We're all doin' fine. I'm very sorry to hear about your grandmother, she was a right nice lady," they said.

"Thank you very much, she was a right nice lady," Parker said sadly and sighed.

"Constable Clark, Constable Weaver if you don't make this Amazon put us down, I'll see to it that you're sacked," David snarled.

"Now David we will have Lady Parker put you down then we'll take you back to the station. Then you can call your solicitors and your parents, then they can come and get you and your friends out of trouble again," Constable Clark said.

"Lady Parker could you please put them down?" Constable Clark asked.

"I sure can," Parker said and dropped them. As soon as their feet hit the floor they were led away.

"Do you think they'll get out as fast as they did last time?" I asked.

"Probably when you have money and power behind you, well you can do whatever you please and get away with it. If you really want my opinion on the matter I think the police believe that since they didn't do anything to you physically they don't see them as a threat to you or anyone else. Now when these three actually hurt someone and it will have to be someone of importance then and only then will they act. But you know Marsh, one of these days they'll get what they deserve. Come on let's go home," Parker said.

We were just wandering through Parker's aunts and uncle's house and we were in the attic. "Wow! Look at this!" Parker exclaimed.

"What is it?" I asked.

"A trunk full of costumes. Hey there's another one!" Parker yelled.

We went through the items and ended up dressing up. Well I did most of the dressing up; nothing fit Parker because of her size. She's tall, thin, heavy chested and big boned, so she just put on wigs and some capes.

"Marsh, you don't even look like you. You could be a spy," Parker said and she laughed.

"Oh brother," I said and we both laughed some more.

"Marsh do you want to come with me tomorrow?" Parker asked.

"I don't know, I've been thinkin' about stayin' here because you'll be gone all day won't you?" I asked.

"Yeah, the way it sounds I'm gonna be in meetings all day, every day of the week. You know you're welcome," Parker said.

"I know but I'll be in the way, so I'll stay here with those beautiful books. So don't worry about it," I said.

Parker left early the next morning. I ran upstairs and went through the costumes. I put one on and looked in the mirror, there was no way they would recognize me. I went to the kitchen and found a very thin bladed knife. "This will work."

With my disguise, my large bag, sharp knife and list I was off to find Billy. Since Parker took the new car they saw us in, I took the older one. I had only been looking for him for twenty-five minutes when I found him!

I parked the car and got out. I made sure he saw me and I walked to an abandoned building with Billy following me at a respectful distance. He made sure no one was around and in he came.

"Hey baby, come on let's have some fun," Billy said.

"What kind of fun?" I asked in a voice that wasn't mine.

"This kind," he said and he pulled out a bag of white powder.

"First you have to catch me!" I exclaimed and took off.

He chased me for a few minutes and I was finally able to get behind him. I found a pipe and I swung it with a force greater than I knew I had. I hit him in the head so hard it cracked open sending pieces of his brain flying through the air.

Once I made sure he was dead I took the baggie from his body and dumped it on him. I made sure I left nothing of me at the crime scene. This took longer than I had expected but I had been in several areas of the building. When I was satisfied it was clean I left.

I went to the door and looked around to make sure no one was outside; when I was satisfied I was alone I left the building. I made my way back to the car and made it back to the house without being seen. I pulled into the garage unnoticed by all; since it was Monday everyone was at work or school.

I put the knife up. I went upstairs and put the costume up. I went to my room and took a long bath and some of the dirt they put on me came off. When I was done I went to the library got a book and curled up to enjoy it.

The ringing phone woke me up. "Hello? Oh hi Parker. I fell asleep trying to read a book. What's up? Yeah, I'd love to meet you. Sure I'll be there in about twenty minutes," I said and hung up.

We had a great lunch and when it was done Parker went back to her meetings and I drove back to the house. By the time I got there the rain had stopped and the sun was starting to come out. It was so nice I decided to take a walk. I just walked without purpose. I didn't realize I had company until I found myself in a secluded area of the park.

It was a deep dark glen with a small creek running through it. My two friends split up and I was able to come up behind Frank and he went the way of Billy, now for David.

I put on my gloves, put my hair under a hat and searched Frank. I found a switchblade and popped it open. I took off so David wouldn't find Frank's lifeless body. "Where are you, you dirty little bitch!" David called.

I threw a rock in front of David. When he turned around I snuck up behind him and slit his throat. He turned around to face me and his eyes opened wide with shock. I made sure no blood could get on me because it was spurting out like a fountain. "I'm here David," and I drove the knife into his eye. I pulled the knife out and I castrated him.

"Well David you'll never hurt anyone again, "I said in another woman's voice.

On the way out of the park I checked on Frank. I wanted to make sure he would never hurt anyone again. I picked up a large rock and threw it on his face. Satisfied they were dead I left the park unnoticed, I made it back to the house, cleaned up and sat back down to read my book. All traces of the dirt I felt on me were gone.

"My god it's pouring!" Parker said.

"You're kiddin'. I must have dozed off again. How'd it go today?" I asked.

"It took longer because they had to explain everything to me. You want to come and have some fun and excitement tomorrow," Parker said and we both started laughing.

We ate, talked some and then turned in. Sometime during the night the fire that was burning inside the abandoned building consumed Billy's body. When the walls collapsed all trace of the crime was erased.

The rain just kept coming down harder and harder. During the night the creek became a raging torrent. The bodies of Frank and David were washed out into one body of fast moving water after another until there was absolutely no trace of them. They would never be a threat to any woman ever again.

CHAPTER EIGHT
POSSESSION

The week passed quickly and on Thursday evening there was a little blurb in the paper about the disappearance of three local men. "Marsh take a look at this. The three that tried to kidnap you are missin'. I'm surprised the police haven't paid you a visit yet, they came to see me today, we talked they were satisfied and they left," Parker said.

"Good, I'm glad to hear that they don't think you had anything to do with it, but them being missin', well that's no loss at all. I hope they're dead, I know that's terrible but that's how I feel I got a call from the police, we talked and they were satisfied I didn't have anything to do with it," I said.

"Good I'm glad they're satisfied, I'm sure the list of people wanting to hurt them is a very long one," Parker said.

Then on Friday there was a bigger write up. "Parker here's another article on those three scum bags. They sure weren't angels. Several girls and women have come forward and told their stories of abduction, abuse, torture, rape and sodomy. Ooh they were nasty bad," I said.

"It also says that they were also into the drug scene. They were sellin' to kids! Can you imagine, good lord they must have had some terrific power behind them. They were also thieves and they were linked to several arsons," I said.

"Marsh you were so lucky to have escaped that van, you could have been another in a long line of women who didn't get justice. Talk about princes among men, I hope their parents finally realize how nasty their sons were. They must have crossed the wrong person or the wrong group of people," Parker said.

"That's what the police think. It also says that they were into so many illegal dealings they don't have a lack of suspects," I said.

"Well they probably won't ever be found, too bad for the parents never knowin' exactly what happened to them. But when you're a bad seed it always comes back to bite you. Are you all packed?" Parker asked.

"Yeah. Is the taxi here?" I asked.

"Yeah. I got our train tickets. Once we get there, Gerald will pick us up. Do you think I have enough film, paper, ink and flash drives?" Parker asked as she lifted up two very large bags.

"Oh yeah, you're set on that point. You ready?" I asked.

"Yep, let's go," Parker said as we went out to our taxi.

We made it to our train and we found our seats and settled in. "Parker are you gonna have to live at Briargate?" I asked.

"No. I should be able to run it from home. Gerald and Sarah will live there as they always have and will keep me informed so will Mr. Barlowe. But I still have to take these stupid pictures for insurance purposes," Parker said and made a face.

"It won't be that bad and I'm sure Gerald and Sarah won't be offended," I said.

"Well I hope you're right. I sure don't want to start out on the wrong foot with them. I don't want them to think I don't trust them because that's so far from the truth. I don't want them to leave me, I really do like them and consider them family just like you are," Parker said, squeezed my hand and sighed.

"Everything will work out, you'll see. Thanks Parker," I said and squeezed back.

The train pulled into the station and there were Gerald and Sarah. "Gerald, Sarah, I'm so glad to see you!" Parker exclaimed and hugged them.

"Miss Parker, we're so glad you're back," Sarah said and almost started to cry.

"Miss Marsha nice to see you also," Gerald said.

"Nice to see you also," I replied.

"Come ladies, let's go before the rain starts," Gerald said.

We had a great meal but something was bothering Parker and I knew what it was. "Gerald, Sarah oh crud," she stammered.

"You're not lettin' us go are you?" Sarah asked.

"Oh no, no, not at all. I have to take inventory of everything and I don't want you to think I don't trust you because I do but Mr. Barlowe says I have to, it's a formality. Please forgive me," Parker said and sucked in a great breath.

"Miss Parker, never in our lives would we think that. Mr. Barlowe insisted we do inventory at least once a year," Gerald said.

"What a relief. I sure wish he would have told me it was a yearly thing. I sure wouldn't have wasted my time worrying about it. What a relief!" Parker sighed.

After the meal we started our rounds. "Parker do you want to split up?" I asked.

"Sure if you want to," Parker said and we split up.

I was snapping picture after picture, I sure don't know why I have to do this. I'm sure Parker isn't doing any of this; she's always been very lazy and gets people to do her work. The longer I thought about it the madder I got. I threw my camera down and stomped off to our room; of course I ran into Parker, the flash from her camera going off startled me.

"Hey Marsh, how's it goin'?" Parker asked.

"It's not I'm tired and I'm tired of doin' your work. So I'm goin' to bed," I snapped.

"Marsh what's wrong with you? Are you alright?" Parker asked with alarm.

"No I'm not alright; I'm tired of doin' your job for you. You've really changed since you got your inheritance. You're actin' like you're some big shot! You know what I don't like you anymore. Your kind makes me sick! I'm goin' home!" I screamed. I left the hallway and a very stunned Parker in the hopes that I could make them believe I went upstairs to get my things.

I grabbed my purse, my pack with my precious items in it and snuck out of the house. By the time they figure it out I'll be long gone.

"Marsh, Marsh, Marsha!" I yelled and ran up to the room and threw open the door.

"Damn," I snapped.

"Is she there miss?" Gerald asked.

"No, where in the heck did she get to. Sarah did you see her?" I asked.

"No miss I didn't," Sarah cried.

"Oh shoot. I know what she did," I cried and bolted down the stairs and in through the kitchen where the open door awaited me.

I ran outside and yelled, "Marsh, Marsha!" and then it hit me, she was no longer in control.

"Gracie come back! Please bring Marsh back!" I pleaded but I knew there'd be no answer. My very best friend, my sister and then Granny Charlotte's words which had been in the back of my mind slammed to the forefront. When family that is not family is in dire need, you will know what to do. But I didn't know what to do or how to get her back. Gracie got what she wanted which was to live again and for now I didn't know what to do or what I could do.

I came back in; I was sobbing; huge racking sobs. I was heartbroken and so angry that I hadn't seen the takeover coming; it seemed to have come out of the blue. For some reason it felt as if another entity had a hand in Marsh's vanishing. "Miss what happened?" Sarah asked but Gerald shook his head at her.

"No Gerald, that's okay, I'll try to explain. As you know I'm blessed with the ability to talk to dead people," and I paused trying to figure out how to put this.

"Well heck Marsh's great, great well anyway her Aunt Gracie was a very close friend of Rosy Whipnickly. When Rosy left she left her diary detailing the killin' of the prostitutes of White Chapel. Gracie became obsessed with it and the diary took her over. Now Gracie has taken Marsh away and I don't know if I'll ever be able to get her back," I snarled and I slammed my fist down on the table splintering it.

"Oh my god I'm so sorry. I can't seem to do anything right today," I moaned.

"Miss please don't worry about it. It was a piece of junk twenty years ago and should have been thrown out. It's not a loss. Can you go on?" Sarah asked and I nodded my head.

"I warned Marsh several times. I thought I had Gracie put away in a safe place, but I guess I was wrong. But what I don't understand is how Gracie got Marsh without me knowin' or sensing it. I know I can turn it off but I should have been able to pick it up. All I can think of is I've failed Marsh, Gracie is extremely strong and I have a feelin' that she had help," I said.

"Miss what are we going to do?" Gerald asked.

"Where will she go?" Sarah asked.

"I don't know on both counts. I don't know what to do; I just don't know what to do. Why couldn't I have figured it out?" I moaned.

"Parker," Penelope said and Gerald and Sarah jumped out of their chairs.

"As you know Gracie is gone. She fed off Marsha's fear, hatred, anxiety and jealousy and she grew extremely strong. She is evil and evil can mask itself. The three who attacked Marsha are dead at her hands, thanks to Gracie. I'm sorry Parker she was too powerful and evil, she was able to make the guards disappear."

"Parker you were right, she did have help, a male spirit that has no facial features," Penelope said.

"How do I find her? How do I find the male spirit since he doesn't have facial features?" I asked.

"You can't, not yet. You're not strong enough yet. Only when you're strong enough will you be able to find her, him and cast Gracie out," Penelope said.

"How do I get stronger? What do I have to learn?" I asked.

"You have to find the White Book of Angorline. When you find the book study it, learn it and keep it near you," Penelope said.

"But why couldn't I feel the take over or them? I can feel others, I feel as if I'm losin' my powers," I said.

"Because they're evil and you're young. You're not losin' your powers, in fact you're gettin' stronger every day. The book will teach you how to use all of your powers to find the ones who don't want to be found. When you find the tall man under the pyramid of light your quest will be close at hand," Penelope said.

"The tall man, pyramid of light how in the heck am I gonna figure this out?" I moaned.

"Parker as soon as you relax and let all fall away the answers will start to fall into place. Now I have to go," Penelope said and she was gone.

"Crud," I said and stomped on the table.

"Miss Parker,"

"Please call me Parker, both of you. There is no reason to call me Miss," I said.

"Alright then, Parker it is. May I speak freely?" Gerald asked.

"Sure, you don't have to ask," I said.

"We, Sarah and I, aren't as educated as some of you, but we will help you in any way we can," Gerald said.

"Gerald, Sarah just because you haven't gotten a college education doesn't matter. You two have a natural wisdom and I appreciate it. And yes I'd be thrilled if you'd help me," I said and hugged them.

"Tomorrow we'll take you to the other library where all the ancient texts are kept. Maybe you'll find a clue," Sarah said and handed me a cup of tea.

I grabbed my pack and purse then ran into the darkness shielded by the rain and fog; I never looked back. I caught the train and back to London I went.

I found a hotel and checked in under my mother's maiden name. Since I had my disguise on nobody would be able to recognize me. I was safe and I knew it. I was safe from the prying eyes of all people especially from Parker. How could I have ever thought she was my friend?

So I sat down and made my plans. The first one on my list was Trevor, there was no way he was going to cheat me again. I might not be able to get my items back but by god he wasn't going to get another scrap of paper from me!

I was going to France to catch a flight home. I did this in case nosy Parker was looking for me. So my plan was to get a good night's sleep, have a light breakfast and then take the train to France. From there I'd get the first flight out, put my affairs in order and I'd travel, that is after I took care of Trevor.

CHAPTER NINE
ESCAPE

I finally escaped from my kidnapper and now I was on my way home, I was so happy I could cry. How did I ever think Parker and I were like sisters let alone best friends, but she has a way about her. She can ingrain herself into your life and then she has you. I've been under her spell since we were six months old.

I actually thought about going to the police and pressing charges against Parker for kidnapping me and for the murder of my family. With that thought on my mind for some reason I pulled out my diary on the first page it said, "No Parker didn't murder your family. She didn't kidnap you. If you press charges all that would do would call attention to you and our plans. It will also alert Parker and she will come and get us." So I did what my diary, my bible said and I let it drop for the moment.

I caught the train and was in France in what seemed like the blink of an eye. I was in no mood to tour Paris or even go to a hotel; I just wanted to go home. So I went straight to the airport and would camp out there until I could get a flight out. I was pleasantly surprised to find out that there was a flight in two hours and it wasn't full, so with my ticket in hand I sat down to wait.

I actually let out a sigh of relief when the plane was in the air. The woman next to me gave me a look and told me flying wasn't that bad and went back to her book. Part of me still expected to see that nosey Parker get on the plane with Gerald and Sarah and try to get me off here by force if need be.

I closed my eyes and when I opened them we were five minutes from landing. As soon as the plane landed I raced to the rental car counters. I paid extra for the company to pick the car up at my house. When all the details were worked out I left the airport and drove straight home. While I was waiting I got all my important papers together, made some phone calls to the utility companies and to Mr. Boyd, my attorney. I told him I had some business I had to attend to and that business was going to keep me away from town for a while.

I called the school and was able to make arrangements with them so I could continue my classes via the internet; all I had to do was sign some papers. I also concealed my cell phone and would get a pre-paid phone because they couldn't trace me.

As soon as I finished my last phone call the rental car people arrived; as they left so did I. I went to school and filled out all the necessary forms. When that was done I went to the bank and closed out the smallest of my accounts of $150,000 and I was set.

With my bags packed I left my ancestral home, I had to pull over because I was crying so hard. As soon as I settled down I headed for Derby Crown. There were several things I had to do once I got there; I had to set up a mail drop for a few weeks, buy a new car and wait for the plates to come in. While I waited for them I made my plans to deal with Trevor when that was done I was going to move on to greener pastures.

I might have slept an hour if I was lucky. I couldn't get Marsha's outburst out of my head. It also bothered me that I couldn't sense the takeover. "Crud, I'm gettin' up!" I snapped at the walls.

I got dressed and went up to the library where the portrait had been moved. I looked at it and there stood Sir Phillip, Penelope who was pregnant again and their four children; two sets of twins. I smiled at them knowing that Penelope was so very happy, she would never grow old and die, I was so happy for her and I wiped my tears away.

I said good bye and left the room. I moved the portrait before we left, no way was I going to have my sister and her family live in a closet. I finally left the room unaware that I had been there for two hours. I was pacing up and down every staircase in the house. If Gerald and Sarah weren't awake before I'm sure they are now. I was looking out one of the windows, when I turned around I ran into Gerald, I just about knocked him down. "Gerald I'm so, so sorry, I didn't hear you! Are you alright?" I asked.

"Yes Parker I am. Have some tea and biscuits with me and Sarah. You'll feel better and be able to think better with some food in your stomach."

"Thank you Gerald. I can't tell you how much you and Sarah mean to me," I said and hugged him. I finally let him go and we went to the kitchen to eat breakfast.

"Parker do you want anything else?" Sarah asked.

"Oh no thank you. I'm full and I'm tellin' you it was delicious! Is it too early to go to the other library?" I asked.

"Let me clean up and we'll take you there," Sarah said as she started to clear the table.

"Let me help you," I said and I thought Sarah was going to faint.

"Well now Parker that isn't necessary," Sarah said.

"Oh yes it is. Mom always says if you have chores or a job to do, it makes you a better person. Where is the library?" I asked as I put the plate Sarah handed me into the dishwasher.

"It's below the carriage house and goes on for miles. If you two are done, let's start the tour," Gerald said.

"How many people know about this?" I asked.

"Three. You, me and Sarah. We would have taken you sooner but we couldn't because Miss Marsha was here. Our instructions were from Lady Marjorie, she said you were to go in with us or alone," Gerald said.

"You mean Mr. Barlowe doesn't even know about this place. How'd that happen?" I asked.

"Because Lady Marjorie said even though she trusted Mr. Barlowe with her legal affairs she didn't trust him with her family secrets because he sometimes talked too much," Sarah said. I found this funny, my Grandmother wouldn't trust her lawyer but she trusted these two. But Grandmother was always like that; Gerald and Sarah were as much her family as I was. They would have earned her trust over years of service with her household. Now they would work for me and I know I could trust them with my life just as I do my parents and the quads.

"Should I change lawyers? Did Grandmother say anything else about Mr. Barlow?" I asked.

Before Gerald or Sarah could say anything Grandmother said, "Parker he is the absolute best at what he does. When he was a younger man and he inherited his clients from his father he had a bit of a drinking problem."

"A very dear friend of mine had just purchased a fabulously ugly and extremely expensive necklace. She had it on one day when she went to see him and one thing led to another. She told him everything about it and he got a little into a bottle and let everything come tumbling out."

"Several days later she was robbed. His clients were leaving in droves when his father called. I stormed into his office and took him to task. He hasn't had a drop to drink since then because I talked to all his clients and convinced them to come back, which they did."

"But the main reason I don't want him to know is because I do not want outsiders to know what our family has collected and saved from destruction over the years."

"Only three people at a time know about our treasure. Gerald and Sarah know as did their parents. Parker you are never to say a word about this to anyone. When Gerald and Sarah can no longer care for you and the house they will come to you with their replacements. All of this is in the papers you have with you."

"Now Parker you mustn't blame yourself about your friend. In life Gracie practiced the black arts and became extremely powerful after her death. When you find the White Book and you learn all there is to learn from it, you will be able to defeat Gracie. You will be able to find the faceless spirit and do what needs to be done to free Marsha."

"Parker I am truly sorry for not really giving you my love, all my love as I did Penelope, when you were younger. I must tell you even if Penelope would have stayed, you my dear would still have received Briargate because you are the chosen one," Grandmother said and disappeared.

"What was that all about? The chosen one?" I asked.

"Yes miss, you are the chosen one because of your feelings about this old place. You love and cherish it. Those that have lived here and still visit here called your name just as they did your grandmother. Now if you'd like we'll take you to the library," Sarah said.

"Thank you, thank you both for everything. It will be interesting to see who will be next after me. I'm ready and can't wait," I said and off we went. As we walked all I could think about was how a house could pick it's next caretake so to speak. I don't know why I ever had that thought on my mind, as you can see we aren't you're average run of the mill family.

"Derby Crown, home for a few months. Now let's find us a new home," I said to the stray dog I found on the side of the road. He was a medium sized, speckled hound of some sort. I'm a sucker for dogs and when I saw him it was love at first sight.

We were stopped by some road construction and I looked at the dog and he looked at me. "I think I'll call you Hank. What do you think?" and he winked at me.

"Alright Hank let's go find us a new place to live," I said and it was our turn through the construction.

I found a very nice rental and off I went to the car lots. After the sixth lot I finally found the perfect vehicle, a very nice, one owner, low mileage dark blue Grand Cherokee. It was as they say owned by a little old lady that only drove it to church on Sunday. This one was exactly as advertised; it was something I wouldn't normally have looked at let alone buy.

I finally got Trevor on the phone, as greedy as he is I would have thought he would have been eager and ready to jump at the chance to meet with me. We arranged a meeting and it was decided that I'd pick him up and take him to my house. Since I had everything cancelled, there wouldn't be anyone around except the caretaker. His only job would be to take care of the lawn and make sure everything was closed, locked up tight and not bothered in any way.

I pulled up in front of Trevor's place, it was so dark no one noticed me. Once I was in his apartment I was able to look at his desk. I found his day planner which I put in my bag along with any information pertaining to me.

"Marsha you look very nice. That's a very good look for you. I like it. Are you ready to go?" Trevor asked.

"Yes I am and thank you for your compliments. Come on let's go," I said.

The drive to the house was uneventful. "Marsha are you movin'?" Trevor asked.

"No, I've got some business to attend to. There are several pieces in the basement I'd like you to look at," I said and led the way downstairs.

There were six very nice dressers sitting on several large pieces of plastic. "Marsha these are absolutely marvelous but why are they on this plastic?" Trevor asked.

"The basement has a leak in it and I don't want them gettin' wet," I said.

Trevor was walking in and around the furniture, caressing them greedily when he finally noticed the large plastic sheets hanging from the ceiling. The hanging sheets were under the ones on the floor making it almost as if it were an unbroken sheet of plastic. "Marsha what's this for?" Trevor asked.

"To catch the blood," I said in another voice and ran the very sharp knife across his throat severing his carotid artery.

There was blood all over the place; I almost threw up. But the slit throat was just the beginning. I sliced his face from the corner of his mouth through his cheeks all the way to his ears.

The next step was to castrate him and put it in his mouth. I gutted him like a fish and when all my work was done I rolled him up and taped the bag closed. I pulled him to a dolly and pushed him to my vehicle and drove him to the grave I dug earlier.

This grave was on my property far away from prying eyes. I stopped, dropped him in, covered him up and drug a downed tree over it. Once I was satisfied with my handiwork, I got in, picked up Hank and drove back to Derby Crown.

Gerald and Sarah led me to the carriage house and took me into the office. I sucked in a breath of air and clutched my throat when I pulled my hand away there was blood. "Parker, Parker, oh my god! Gerald what do we do?" Sarah screamed.

"I'll be fine, let me sit down for a minute. Can I get a towel?" I asked.

"Here you go Parker. What happened?" Gerald asked as he touched the long red welts that were starting to form on my face.

"Gracie has claimed her fourth victim, in this newest murder spree. His name is damn he's gone," I said as I wiped the last of the blood from my neck.

"Parker are you alright? Those look like they hurt," Sarah said and wiped her eyes.

"Sarah please don't cry, they don't hurt, they're just nasty lookin' and they took me by surprise. It's imperative now more than ever that I find that book," I said.

"If you're sure then we'll continue," Gerald said as Sarah led me to the large workbench that was on the wall in front of me.

She put my finger on a button and then pressed my finger on that button. I heard a click and then I heard something grate. I turned around and was startled by the movement of the smaller workbench.

The cement floor that the smaller free-standing workbench was on slowly started to swing open revealing an opening. "Merciful Mary, this is fantastic!" I exclaimed.

"Come along Parker," Gerald said and led the way with a torch.

Once we got down the stairs he flipped a switch and the lights on the walls blazed revealing a vast hall of treasures. "Oh my god above!" I exclaimed with awe.

"Isn't it grand? They put the lights in, in the early 30's. They updated them about ten years ago," Sarah said.

"How did they do it, if only three people at a time know about it?" I asked.

"I did the light upgrade, my father and grandfather did it before me. You see miss, I mean Parker, we all have treasures in here. Lady Marjorie, god rest her soul, was exceedingly kind and generous to us," Gerald said.

"She would give us bonuses and we'd go on holiday to many exotic locations where we'd buy beautiful things. Some of them were rare and priceless. When we would get home our treasures were put in here," Sarah said.

"And now Parker you're in charge and you can now put your treasures in here also," Gerald said.

"I know exactly what will go in here. It's a diary and until I make a decision as to its future it will be safe in here. Do you have many books down here?" I asked.

"Yes Parker we do. In special climate-controlled vaults. My father and Gerald installed them. This is a monument to him, he was killed before he could put the finishing touches on it; Gerald had to finish it," Sarah said.

"I'm sorry Sarah," I said.

"It's alright Parker; it's been sixteen years since that day. Now I have wonderful memories," Sarah said and once again we started our trek.

"Here we are. Marvelous isn't it?" Gerald asked and all I could do was shake my head in agreement.

We went in and put on some cotton gloves and I started to lovingly touch the spines of these ancient books and then there were the scrolls. Some of these scrolls were from the library of Alexandria! What treasures were here and I was going to get to know each and every one of them!

"Gerald, Sarah do you know if there's a catalog of books?" I asked.

"Yes Parker there is, it's in the library under lock and key. We have a hard copy and several discs which are on our list of things to put on flash drives," Sarah said.

"I think I'm gonna have to look at it. I'll never be able to find anything," and I stopped.

"What did you find?" Sarah asked.

"Hopefully some information about the White Book and Angorline. Is there a desk or anything? Never mind I see them. Do you mind if I sit and look through this?" I asked.

"Parker we don't mind and you don't have to ask. When you're done just give us a call, there's a house phone on the desk and we'll come get you. Now we'll leave you to study," Gerald said.

I sat at that table for several hours and I learned many helpful things. Angorline was a real person, he wasn't a myth. He was highly regarded by several ancient rulers and is mentioned in several texts, there were several references to his biography and his biographer.

With my notes finished I called the house and within minutes Sarah appeared. I was going to meet her and head up the stairs but she closed the door behind her. "Come this way Parker. That's the entrance only, if you try to go that way I've heard stories passed down from one caretaker to another that very bad things happen if you go out the way you came in. We'll have to take a little walk to the exit," Sarah said.

"Ooh sounds good to me. I get to see some more of this wonderful place," I said.

"This is one of several exits," Sarah said and put my hand on a small lever. I pulled it down, the door slid open and we stepped into the old servant's kitchen. As soon as we were in the door slid shut behind us.

I made sure I didn't call any attention to me or Hank, my goal was to be invisible; to stay off the radar. The missing posters of Trevor started to appear, because of my dealings with him I made sure I contacted the authorities, I fed them my false story which they believed without question. And why wouldn't they, I've never done anything wrong in my life. The only contact I've had with the police was with Billy, David and Frank and I was the victim. Since my statement led them nowhere and with nothing to go on, Trevor's case went cold.

My new license plates finally arrived and my two weeks of waiting were well spent. I had compiled a list of people who spent their lives hurting people. On my list were sexual predators, con men, dead beat dads, paroled criminals and those that were guilty but were let off on technicalities.

The first person on my list was Abbigail Gustavian. She was arrested for the murder of her year-old daughter. She said she left the baby upstairs to answer the front door. While she was away the baby fell through the railings of the stairs and was killed.

The jury was deadlocked and went over the evidence for two weeks. They put her on trial again and the jury deadlocked again. Once again she was put through another trial and once again they were deadlocked. Finally it was decided that they wouldn't put her on trial again, so she was released and the case was dropped; justice was definitely not carried out. I was going to make sure the baby finally got justice.

"Come on Hank, we're heading to Vista Bell where justice will be carried out," I said happily and out the door we went.

CHAPTER TEN
PUNISHMENT RECEIVED

"Well Hank let's see if Abbigail still lives here. Now you stay here, guard the Jeep and be good. I'll see if I can get a room and some information. I'll be back as soon as I can," I said. I gave Hank a hug and a kiss; good god I love this little dog more than any other pet I've had.

"Well good morning. How are you this fine day?" the owner of the motel said.

"I'm fine thank you. How are you?" I asked.

"Just dandy. How can I help you?" she asked.

"Well I need a room for a few days and I have a medium sized dog. He's a good boy and won't be any problem," I said.

"Not a problem, I have three labs so I give a discount to dog lovers," the owner said.

"Really that's very nice. Have you ever had damage?" I asked.

"So far, knock on wood, not at all. Now do you want smoking or no smoking, what floor do you want and do you want a full, queen or king size bed?" the owner asked.

"Thank you. Third floor, king, non-smoking and I'll be here oh I think five days. I'm lookin' to move away from an abusive boyfriend," I said.

"Well my dear, you've come to the right place. Your room is 306 and because you've had a rough time of it, I'm givin' you my special discount. That will be $175 for your entire stay," she said.

"Oh my, you're so very kind. Thank you so very much," I said and started crying.

"Now child just dry your eyes and relax. You'll be fine; I'll make sure of it. Now you take a deep breath and fill out this form while I get your key ready. I'll give you some extra towels and blankets. By the way my name is Aggie," she said and stuck out her hand.

"Thanks Aggie my name is Bobbie, very nice to meet you," I said and grabbed her hand.

"Here yah go Bobbie. Now you go get settled and if you need anything just give me a call, I'm here all the time," Aggie said.

"Thanks Aggie, thanks for everything," I said, took my stuff and went back to the Jeep.

Once in the room with Hank I put my things away and grabbed the phone book. Sure enough Abbigail was still listed, now all I had to do was find out about her without calling attention to myself. I didn't want to be noticed for asking questions.

"Sarah before I look at the inventory do you think I could get something to eat. I don't want you to think I'm lazy but I don't want you to think I'm takin' over your kitchen. And would you mind if I'd come down and fix something to eat, oh say at midnight," I said.

She started to laugh, "Parker that's a good one. You worry too much about these things. This is your house; you can come and go as you please. If you want to come down here at midnight you can come down here at midnight or any other time," Sarah said and I felt a little bit better.

"Well I have to worry about something other than Marsh. I feel so helpless but I know that won't help Marsh, I have to be strong and I have to live as normally as possible, so can we eat?" I asked, smiled and we all started to laugh.

"Boy was that good, thank you very much. Sarah you're a terrific cook," I said and my next stop was the library.

I was now the proud owner of some great and priceless titles, but for now I was only interested in the books regarding Angorline that we had. I searched the internet and found several very interesting articles which I printed.

"Gerald where's the nearest library and are there any bookstores that specialize in ancient books?" I asked.

"The nearest good-sized library is Brookstone and there are several bookstores there. I can take you there tomorrow, we'll leave early so you can get there when they open," Gerald said.

"Are you sure you don't mind driving? Because if you have things to do, I can drive myself," I said and Gerald started to chuckle.

"Parker it's not any trouble, it's my job. You must remember this is your estate and we work for you. Besides that it is our day to go into town for supplies," Gerald said.

"Parker if we have time how would you like to go for a picnic?" Sarah asked.

"That would be absolutely terrific! I was gonna suggest that also!" I said and we all laughed.

"Well then it's all settled and I can't wait. If you'd excuse me I'm gonna work on those pictures for Mr. Barlowe," I said and walked off with the weight of the world hanging around my neck.

I stopped back at the office, "Aggie can you recommend any areas that are inexpensive to live but nice?" I asked.

"Well let me think. Well there are a lot of very nice homes on 89th and Sharpe. People are movin' out left and right because of that damned Abbigail Gustavian," Aggie snapped.

"Who? What did she do?" I asked pretending I had no clue.

"Abbigail Gustavian. She killed her daughter," Aggie said.

"Oh I remember her now. But they let her go, something about a hung jury," I said.

"They had three trials and all of them ended in a hung jury. The last one; there were three that said the state didn't prove their case beyond a shadow of a doubt. I sat in on some of the proceedings and what I found very disturbing was the way these three people sat there and looked at her; it was as if they worshipped her. Well if they would have taken the jury to her house and let them look at the railings," and I cut Aggie off.

"Didn't anyone else notice their behavior? Why didn't they go there?" I asked.

"I don't know I even caught up with the lead prosecutor and mentioned it to her. All she did was tell me to mind my own business and if she saw me there again she would have me arrested," Aggie said and I couldn't believe it.

"You have got to be kiddin' me. That woman should be disbarred and prosecuted," I said.

"Well that won't happen, the day after the trial ended she was found dead in her home. There were all sorts of rumors flying around but they ruled it a suicide. Well back to the railings. They were conveniently destroyed and new ones put in before the trial started. Anybody with any sense knew that little girl couldn't have fallen through there. Her mother pitched her over the railing and the same or worse should happen to Abbigail," Aggie snapped.

"You don't want to say that because if something does happen the police will be knockin' at your door. Do you have a map of the town?" I asked.

"Yes I do, here keep this one and I won't spout off anymore," Aggie said and handed me the map.

"Thanks, I'll see you later," I said and out I went in search of Abbigail.

It was just a ten-minute drive from my motel and it was very easy to find Abbigail. Her windows were boarded up and graffiti marked her house, garage and lawn. The houses on either side of hers were empty so were the two directly in front of her.

There were six others near hers that were for sale and five that were for rent. So I pulled in front of the empty ones and pretended to be looking at them. I would be able to get a very good feel of her without causing suspicion.

I walked to the first rental and to my shock it was unlocked. I went in with the brochure in my hand and started my tour.

I had a perfect view of Abbigail's house. As I was watching the front door opened and out she stepped. I checked my watch 4:04 p.m. and I made a note of that. She walked to the garage, got in the car and took off to the east.

I walked across the street to look at her house, get a better feel for it. I went down the driveway of the house for sale and was able to see that the back door was slightly ajar.

"Can I help you miss," and I almost jumped off the driveway.

"Oh shoot officer you scared the livin' daylights out of me. I was just lookin' for rentals and I couldn't help myself, this house is beautiful! I'm sorry I didn't mean to trespass. I won't do it again," I said.

"Don't worry about it miss; you're not in any trouble. We just have to keep an eye on this place. So we patrol each day at eight in the morning and four in the afternoon. Have a nice day," and he tipped his hat at me.

"Officer would you recommend this neighborhood for me to move into?" I asked.

"Well you could get a place extremely cheap. But you'd be livin' in a neighborhood with a murderer," he replied.

"Well I'll sure have to think about that information. Thank you very much, I hope you have a good day also," I said and watched him walk off.

Well that was a very interesting bit of information, but then again that doesn't surprise me. For some reason people tell me everything, even if I just met them. So they patrol twice a day, I'll have to keep that in mind when I watch Abbigail. I walked into the empty houses' backyard and was able to see into Abbigail's. There was a park behind her backyard and she had no fence. From there I walked down the sidewalk to the next house and once again made my way to the backyard where I got a better view of Abbigail's yard.

I came out of the backyard and walked across the street to a house that was for sale or rent. Once again the door was unlocked so I went in. I looked out the front windows but couldn't see a thing so I went upstairs. I looked out the windows in the front bedroom, it was a perfect view.

While I was looking out the window Abbigail returned. She was carrying a small bag of take-out food. "Hmm, I wonder, she has to be alone. I'll just have to watch her a little longer," I said to the empty room.

I left the house, got in my Jeep and drove to the park. To my surprise there was a parking lot right in front of the hedge that served as a fence. But Abbigail's yard was the only one that didn't have a fence. I also noticed that several of the homeowners, those that were left, parked back here and went in through their backyard.

I got out of my Jeep and walked to the trash can, I pretended to throw something out so I was able to look into the backyard. "Well what do you know?" I asked a squirrel and went back to the Jeep. I headed back to the motel and decided I'd leave early in the morning so I could get the feel of the neighborhood.

I was up bright and early so bright and early it was still dark outside. So since I was up, I decided to continue my picture taking. I was on the third floor in the east wing when the lights in the green room went on and the door opened.

I went in and there stood Rosy Whipnickly. "Hello Miss MacStuart. It's a pleasure to finally meet you. I've heard so very much about you from your sister and grandmother."

"Well thank you and it's very nice to meet you also. I've heard some nice things about you from Mr. Larkwood. I'm sorry about your mother; she was taken from you too early. Please call me Parker," I said.

"Thank you Parker, please call me Rosy. She is loose and the terror has started. What I did was wrong but I was young, terribly hurt and filled with hatred for my father. He was a brutal, vicious man and inside our house was nothing but pain. He had brutalized and eventually murdered all of my six sisters. The only people he showed actual loving feelings to were the prostitutes. I couldn't do anything to or against my father because he was very wealthy and very well connected. That's the reason I killed, I avenged my mother and sisters and had my revenge on my father. As soon as I killed the last prostitute I threw myself into the river unfortunately I was saved," Rosy said and wiped the tears from her eyes.

"But Gracie is different, she will kill until she is caught or she is killed. She is unstable, even before I showed up and she found my diary, there had been several horrendous murders, all unsolved but she was responsible. The reason I left was because she was obsessed with me and my growing suspicion that she was a murderer wouldn't stop nagging at me. I was almost a prisoner and felt like I did when at home with my father. I couldn't go or do anything without her following me or questioning me."

"I can't count how many times I tried to tell Gracie's family that she needed help, she was unstable and I feared dangerous to herself and others. They were incensed, how dare I, a lowly servant, tell them such things. Gracie came from a good family with good breeding and people of good breeding didn't and wouldn't do such things. It took everything I had in me not to tell them about my family and what we went through and we were a good family."

"They told me that since I was just a servant, hired to take care of the house and to mind my own business. They told me if I ever showed my face again they'd have me arrested. So I left and when I did I left in a terrible hurry, I wanted to leave before Gracie came home, so I had packed ahead of time. The one thing I didn't do was leave my diary, I knew it would only further damage her. I packed my bag and left the room. When I got settled in my new home, my diary was gone," Rosy said.

"But why didn't you go back to get it?" I asked.

"Because that's exactly what she wanted me to do. I knew if I went back to that house, I'd never be seen again. Even if I would have gone back her family would never have let me in. I tried, god knows I tried to tell them and warn them but they turned a deaf ear to my pleas," Rosy said.

"The three that tried to kidnap Marsh and are now missin' are dead at her hands. I know another has met a similar fate but I couldn't see him and I don't know why," I said.

"Trevor is the one you felt and soon another will join him. You will never find her or see the victims until you study the White Book, but you will continue to feel their pain. Parker I'm terribly sorry for your friend, I'm so deeply sorry," Rosy said and was gone.

"Damn it Marsh! Why didn't you fight, you never fight, you always give up too fast," I cried out. I sat down and started to cry. I knew that when I see my friend again I'll have to drive Gracie out and this time I'll have to kill Gracie's evil spirit. My big fear is that the memories of what Gracie did will fill Marsh's head and she won't be strong enough to face them.

"Oh Marsh," I said, wiped my eyes and then continued with my pictures.

I walked around for two more hours until Gerald and Sarah were up. Once breakfast was over we made our lists of what we had to do. When that was done we were off to Brookstone.

My first stop was Bookman's Antiques and Book Shoppe. I opened the door and the bell on the door jingled announcing my presence but the store was empty. I walked in and other than the doors at Briargate this was the only other place I never had to duck down to get through a door. I'm 6' 11" and have grown an inch since the incident at the ice-cream shop, so this was a very interesting find. To me it only meant one thing, the owner is big.

I was alone in the store; I didn't even see a clerk. I could have taken something and ran out of the store and no one would have noticed. I was looking at a very lovely, ornately carved black lacquer box when I heard, "Good morning miss, how may I help you?" I nearly jumped off the floor, it's a good thing I had a good grip on that box or it would have sailed across the room. I might be able to talk to dead people but I sure as heck couldn't sense this man.

I spun around and there stood a very large, very handsome man in his mid to late fifties. He had salt and pepper hair, which he had cut short and very stylish. He had a neatly trimmed goatee which was black as were his eyebrows. And under those black eyebrows behind some of the longest black lashes were piercing blue eyes. I'm sure he has to beat the women off with a stick.

"You startled me! I didn't know you were here. Is this piece for sale?" I asked and marveled at his very large muscular build.

"Yes miss it is. Would you like it?" he asked in a deep bass voice.

"Yes I would, thank you," I said and followed him to the counter.

"Is there anything else?" he asked and before I could answer the largest man I have ever seen stepped into the room. He was well over seven feet tall; I'm sure he was closer to seven and a half feet tall. He had shoulders you wouldn't believe and his chest, holy crud it was huge and his knit shirt stretched tight across it; my knees turned to mush. He has the hairiest arms I have ever seen on a man and when he raised his arm to brush some dust off his face his muscles bulged, I thought his shirt sleeve would explode. He was also the spitting image of the older man. My hope and the thought was that I had found the tall man but there was no pyramid of light.

"Yes there is. I was wondering if you had any material on Angorline," I asked.

"Yes miss I do. Come this way," he said, gave his very large relative a nod and he left the room. He then turned to me, took my elbow and escorted me to the next room.

I half expected to find the White Book of Angorline because of the tall man but it was not to be. "Here we go miss, this section deals with Angorline. They are either written about him or written by him," the owner said.

After looking at all the books I finally made my mind up and purchased four that were written by him. I paid for my books and my next stop was the library.

I left early the next morning; I had decided to walk. It wasn't that far and as it turned out it was easier to walk than it was to drive.

I made the rounds of the neighborhood and found it surprisingly quiet. It was 7:00 a.m. and there was very little activity. Well considering thirteen houses were empty, no wonder there wasn't much activity.

I went back to the rental that overlooked Abbigail's house and it was still unlocked. Once I made sure I was alone in the house I went upstairs and began my vigil.

At 7:30 a small red car pulled out from down the street. At 8:00 a black truck drove by followed by the police. At 8:30 Abbigail opened up the front door and looked around. She left the house and headed up the left-hand sidewalk. At 10:30 Abbigail returned from the opposite direction, a white panel van rolled by her and the occupants threw something at her and I could hear them laugh as they sped off.

She ran into the house and slammed the door. She stayed in the house until noon when she drove off. I got a very good look in the garage; there was only one car so I knew she lived alone.

She came back at 1:00 p.m. with another take out bag; this one was from Barney's. I knew Barney's wasn't in Vista Belle, so she goes out of town to get her meals, very interesting.

Abbigail stayed in the house the rest of the afternoon and not one single solitary soul ventured down this street. I stayed in the house with Hank all day and not one person came to the house for any reason.

At 4:00 the police passed slowly by her house and drove out of sight. At 4:30 the small red car came back and pulled into the garage, at 5:00 the black truck drove by me and that was it. At 5:30 Abbigail left her house and she returned at 6:30. At 7:00 I left the house with Hank and no one noticed us.

We crossed to Abigail's side of the street. I walked up the sidewalk passed two houses and found a sidewalk that went toward the park. I followed the sidewalk and ended up in the park. "Well Hank this is very interesting," I said. I walked over to a trash can and threw out the garbage from the food and water I brought for Hank and I today.

Hank and I were back early the next day but we came through the park. I peeked in the backyard and the door was still open. After I confirmed my suspicion we went back to the rental house and settled down.

The routine was the same as the day before. At the end of our second day we went to the park and I parked once again and her door was still open. Why would she leave the door open? Is it for a quick get away? Or is it open to lure people in and become murder victims. I wonder if there's any way I could talk to Aggie without arousing suspicion?

I decided that Thursday would be the day I had tomorrow to do one final day of surveillance. Tomorrow would be different; I was going inside Abbigail's house.

As Hank and I were driving back to the motel a thought came to me. I was going to ask Aggie without being obvious if it was safe to leave doors as well as windows open. I'll broach it by saying I've seen several open. "Hank I've got my plan all figured out," I said happily and rubbed his head.

"Hank I'm gonna go see Aggie but first I'm gonna put you in the room for a minute or two while I talk to her," I said and went to our room.

"Hi Aggie," I said.

"Well hi Bobbie how are you doin'?" Aggie asked.

"I'm fine how are you?" I asked.

"I'm fine what can I do for you?" Aggie asked.

"Well I was wondering how safe it is here. Can I leave my windows and doors open? Are there many murders or disappearances?" I asked.

"Well it was peaceful until Abbigail, damn bitch," Aggie said and fell silent, then she snapped her fingers as she thought of something.

"You know now that I think of it, there have been several people that have disappeared. The police just don't have a clue. So our once safe little city isn't safe anymore," Aggie said sadly.

"Well I'll have to take that into consideration. Thanks Aggie," I said and a customer came in. I waved then left and went back to my room.

"Well Hank very interesting talk with Aggie. I can't wait to see what we'll find," I said happily and fixed our supper.

Wednesday is finally here! I'm so excited! We left early but this time we took the Jeep. I found the perfect place for it and once parked; Hank and I made our way to the rental house. I watched the police and the same two vehicles leave. As soon as Abbigail left I went to her house but I left Hank behind.

I snuck into the house by the open back door and was shocked by the inside. It was filthy, there was garbage strewn all around the house and a horrendous stench filled it. There were rust colored stains on the kitchen floor, I didn't have time to look at it closely, I had other things to do. I was able to navigate through the trash and soggy pieces of flooring by a path snaking through her house. I walked all around the house opening up all the drawers with a towel because everything was covered in crud. I was just looking; I was hoping that I'd find something proclaiming her guilt.

I looked at my watch and had thirty minutes left, so I decided to go upstairs. At the top of the stairs shoved between the railings was a doll with a name tag on it. I looked over the railing on the floor was another doll with a name tag on it.

Once in her room I found the mother lode, it was her diary. How did the police miss this? I opened up the book and found out. "The police think they are so smart, let's see if they can find this in the bird house."

I found something else. "I know I won't go to prison for killin' Mattie because there will be some sympathetic twits on the jury. I could have just thrown her over but I wanted her to suffer. It was so easy to shove her through the railings, I was excited, aroused by her screams of terror. I never wanted that brat anyway. Once my lousy husband found out it wasn't his, he left that's what everyone thinks, they'll never find that bastard. They'll never find those few that came for me, they were so easy to dispose of. Only the map knows there they're at."

I turned the page and sure enough there was a beautifully detailed map. "Oh you little piece of murdering garbage. Don't you worry, you'll get yours," I said, put the book up and made my way out of the house and back to Hank.

"Hello Hankie boy, how are you doin' sweetie? We've got work to do tomorrow. As soon as justice is carried out we'll leave early in the morning before Aggie is awake. I hate to leave her though, she's very nice almost as nice as Rosy," I said and kissed him on the top of his head.

"Thursday, Thursday, Thursday. Today is the day that Abbigail will face justice!" I sang out loud. Once again Hank and I left early in the morning and we staked out Abbigail's house. The day passed slowly and when Abbigail left for her supper I sprang into action. I left Hank in a safe place, snuck inside and waited for Abbigail.

She returned and came in. She went into the living room, sat down and turned on the TV. It was so loud she didn't hear me lock the doors. I walked into the living room and said, "Hello Abbigail. I hope you enjoyed your meal because it's your last one," I said.

"What? Who are you?" she asked.

"I'm the one that's gonna see to it that your daughter gets justice," I said and pulled out my knife.

The first cut got her across the face, she cried out in shock and her eyes widened with fear. The second one cut her neck and the third sliced through her left breast. "Well Abbigail it's been a pleasure playin' with you but I'm bored. It's time for some real fun," I said. With the next cut her arteries were severed in her throat and her head was almost lopped off. When I was done she was dead and justice had been carried out.

When I was done I skipped up the stairs and did a victory dance where Abbigail had murdered her daughter. I went to her room and took out the diary, I'm going to mail it to the police so they can see that they did the right thing and arrested the right person. I made sure that I addressed the package with my left hand so they couldn't compare my handwriting if they ever connected me to the case. I would mail it from one of the places that I'll be traveling through but it has to be a bigger city so that no one would remember me.

I picked up Hank and we went back to the room. I slept for a few hours and at 4:00 a.m., I got up packed the Jeep, dropped the key off and Hank and I were off to our next case of justice.

CHAPTER ELEVEN
HUNTING IS SO MUCH FUN

"Well Hank, next stop Victorville and Phillip Roscoe. You know he was accused of raping one girl and they figured he'd done it to many, many others. Of course he was let off on a technicality because of tainted DNA evidence. But he's gonna meet with justice at our hands," I said and patted Hank's head.

Victorville was one hundred fifty miles from Vista Bell and was the gateway to the Hobnail National Forest. This great forest encompasses hundreds of thousands of acres in three different states. It has world class rivers for white water rafters, caves abound for explorers, sheer rock faces for the rock climbers and thousands of miles of trails, it was a paradise.

It is also the perfect place for a pervert like Phillip Roscoe to prey upon young girls and women. This is where I'll put my next plan into place. I'm going to lure that dirty pervert to a secluded area and once there I'll cut him up as if he were a Thanksgiving turkey.

Hank and I found a cabin in the park. When we were settled in we went for a walk and I got my first look at Phillip Roscoe. If ever there was someone that gave off a bad vibe it was him. He is a tall skinny man with narrow shoulders and a pigeon chest. He is also knock kneed and pigeon toed. He wears thick black framed glasses with tape on the bridge of his nose that magnified his beady little green eyes. He has a straggly red beard and a small scar on his forehead. To make matters even worse he's dirty and smells to high heaven. He looked and smelled as if he hasn't had a bath in weeks.

"Well Hank this could be a smelly mess, but one that has to be done," I said and I caught his attention.

I made my way to the library and the big man from the bookstore was behind me. I just kept walking and he just kept following me, he wasn't even trying to hide it; not that he could hide anyway. I finally had, had enough. I whirled around so fast I caught him by surprise. "Why are you followin' me? And don't you dare tell me you aren't!" I demanded. This might not have been the smartest thing in the world to do considering he was a huge, massive, heavily muscled man. I'm also sure he was perfectly capable of snapping me in half like a pretzel.

"Yes I am following you," he replied in an even deeper bass voice than the older man and then gave me a rakish smile.

"Well why?" I asked.

"Because my uncle asked me to," he replied.

"I ask again, why?" I was growing a little agitated.

"You wouldn't believe me if I told you. By the way my name is James Stuart," he said and stuck out his hand which was huge!

"Well why don't you try tellin' me? My name is Parker MacStuart," I said and stuck out my hand.

"Well here goes. Uncle Robert has told me from before the time I could see over the counter at the book store that I was to help the tall woman who seeks the truth in the White Book and who speaks and sees the dead. Are you she?" James asked.

"Nice to meet you also. Yes I am. How did your uncle know?" I asked.

"Because he gets flashes. They usually come to me,"

"Stop right there. Oh I get it now, I know what you're doin', you big pig, you're hittin' on me and tryin' to get me in your bed," I snapped, thought about slapping him, but decided that would be a very bad idea, pulled away and started to leave.

He grabbed my arm and said, "Behind you on your left is a beautiful older woman, very nicely built, I can see where you get it from. She's dressed all in purple, ramrod straight, salt and pepper hair, matching sliver earrings and necklace," James said.

"That's my Grandmother," I said then I turned around and there she stood.

"Grandmother why are you talkin' to him?" I asked.

"So you would know he speaks the truth. Parker he means you no harm, he will help you if you let him. Now go to the library another has fallen," Grandmother stopped as if too weary to go on.

"I know I felt it. This attack was worse than the first one. My fear is that they'll continue to get worse with each successive attack. That's why I sent her the dog. I'm surprised she doesn't recognize him; he was Mr. Larkwood's dog Buddy. I'm hopin' his devotion to Marsh or Gracie will help somewhat," I said and shrugged.

"I'm sure you will soon feel the pain because another will fall, she is hunting him now. You must be thorough with your studies. Remember when you find the tall man under the pyramid of light your search is almost over," and she was gone.

"Nothing like putting pressure on you. If you'd like me to I'll help you," James said.

"Well if Grandmother says so then okay. Come on let's go, this is urgent," I said and off we went to the library.

Hank and I finally managed to lose Phillip; it only took us the rest of the day and nearly twenty miles. By the time we got back, Hank and I were dragging. I made sure that we had all the supplies in the cabin so we wouldn't have to go back outside. Now wouldn't be a good time to run into Phillip. My plans aren't yet complete besides that I'm so tired I doubt I'd be able to fight him off.

"Hank how about a bite to eat?" I asked and he gave a little woof.

I took a bath and slept fitfully. I kept dreaming and worrying about Phillip. I sure don't want him to gain the upper hand by sneaking up on us. So after about the twentieth time of getting up and checking the door and windows, I lodged a chair under the locked door and put some small pieces of firewood on the windows so they couldn't be lifted. Once that was done I finally fell asleep.

I woke up later than I wanted to but it was still only 8:00 a.m. and I had plenty of time to pick my spot. "Come on Hank, eat up, we've got to go," I said.

We were out of the cabin by 8:30 a.m. with all our supplies. After walking for almost three hours I finally found an area that looked promising. I hadn't seen anybody since we left the parking lot. I felt as if Hank and I were the only ones on the face of the planet. Since there isn't anybody out and about this should be an easy task to find the perfect spot.

We walked up a small hill and off to my left was a lovely grove of trees. "Come on Hank, let's just go and take us a look see," I said.

We walked over to the trees and I noticed there was a natural depression. "Oh this will work just fine. Hank I'm gonna tie you up right here. You let me know if anyone comes near here," I said.

I pulled out my shovel and got in the depression. I was surprised to find out that once in the depression I couldn't be seen. "Oh this is gonna be easier than I thought."

I kept digging and digging until I had a six-foot-deep pit! I climbed out, put my shovel away, looked around to make sure we were alone and we left. Now all I had to do was find Phillip. This place is so large, I'm sure it was just a matter of chance that I had run into him, now I'll see if I can find Phillip, now that I'm looking for him.

James and I entered the library, we both had to duck and all heads turned toward us. "Why are they staring at us?" I asked never giving our height a second thought.

"Because of our size and your beauty," and I shot him a glance; all he did was smile.

"So anyway to see one of us causes heads to turn, to see us together is I'm sure a sight to behold," James said.

"You've got a point there. I get used to it and usually don't give it a second thought," I said.

"Even if you weren't so tall people would still stare at you Miss MacStuart. I said it once and I'll say it again you are a very beautiful woman," James said and I just stared at him and blushed.

"Thank you, I guess. Please call me Parker. Come on let's go start lookin'," I said and I received that rakish smile of his once again.

We walked up and down the aisles of the library when we finally found the section that I needed. There were some of the same books that I've already looked at and through and bought. I kept thumbing through the shelves when I finally found something that could very well be important.

The two books I found actually had passages from the White Book in them. There was one passage that nearly knocked me for a loop. "There will come a day when two who are sisters but not true sisters will be separated by the arrival of the evil one. They younger of the sisters will have to fight for the soul of the older sister. When the evil is defeated the older sister will be saved, happiness will be found but almost lost," and the passage ended.

"I've got to find this book so I can figure out how to get Gracie out of Marsh. Where in the heck is the pyramid of light?" I asked.

"Well there is the glass pyramid in Paris or it could be something to do with light and not a structure at all," James said.

"So you think I might be thinkin' to literally? And if I'm not where am I gonna find another tall man unless you're comin' with me and you're gonna be under a pyramid of light," I said.

"Yeah I do think you're thinking to literally but you might be able to find someone taller than me under the light but the tall man could be a street, a bridge, a park or something like that. You'll just have to keep your eyes open," James said.

"Well you could be right. I'll have to keep my mind as well as my eyes open. Do they let people make copies? And I don't know about finding another tall man, you're huge," I said and he just smiled.

"Sure, what all do you want copied and I'll take care of it," James said.

I marked the pages that I thought would be the most helpful. "You know it's too bad I can't buy these. Mr. Stuart do you know if anybody would have these for sale?" I asked.

"Please call me James. I don't know right off the top of my head. I can check with Uncle Robert. It might take a little while to track down but maybe he can find something," James said.

"Thank you James," I said and handed him the books. I watched him walk off he was so big and so very handsome. I also couldn't get over his movements he walked so silently and with such confidence and for a big man he was actually graceful in his movements. I bet he has to beat the women off with sticks. I'm sure his calendar is always full.

Watching him walk I came to the conclusion that he has to be a spy or an assassin or something along those lines. But then again how could someone as big as he is be invisible like an assassin would have to be. He must be at least seven and a half feet tall or taller. This is the only person I have ever been around that makes me feel small. Built like he is he looks like a man from what could have been in the ancient sagas. He's got muscles on top of muscles and he makes me feel very secure and safe.

"Here you go. I called my uncle and he'll check around. There are a couple of other antique and book stores in town, I can take you there if you like," James said.

"Well why not, let's go," I said and he led the way.

We got two steps out the door when a dyed blonde with implants the size of melons ran up to him shouting, "Jimmy! Jimmy!" She had a little itty-bitty leopard print skirt on, a short black leather jacket and stiletto heels. She jumped up into his arms and wrapped her legs around him; I sure did get a show! She had on a black thong and tattoos on her cheeks. She planted a kiss on him that I felt!

"Holy blue blazes I'll leave you two alone. You need to get a room to finish your business. I'm sure those boys waitin' for the bus are gettin' a thrill lookin' at your bare cheeks!" I snapped and walked off muttering.

Hank and I walked all the way back to one of the four main parking lots, still no sign of him. We started to walk back and forth as if we were looking for our car. The only thing we got for our trouble was sore feet and several nasty glares.

From literally pounding the pavement we meandered into the souvenir shop, the restaurant, the snack shop and the women's bathroom, not one glimpse of him. I did notice that I was on the radar of several other perverts but not the one I wanted. I actually walked up to one who started following me and said, "If I see you around me again I'll cut you up like a fish. Don't you even try to tell me you're not followin' me that line won't work with me. You need to walk away and tell the others what I told you," I hissed.

He swallowed hard and backed up keeping his eyes on me. He did go up to the others and spread the word. I wasn't worried about him being able to describe me, I had on yet another disguise, so let him tell if he dares. I'm sure the police would be very interested in talking with him and the others.

"Come on Hank, let's try another spot," I said and off we went to another parking lot. This search for our elusive, stinky pervert went on all day. When we finally went back to our cabin I swear we traveled about one hundred fifty miles and if we didn't it sure felt as if we did.

This insane search for this pervert went on for four days. Finally on the fifth day, I found him, I was so excited I had to keep from doing cartwheels in the parking lot. "Come on Hank, there he is!" I said excitedly as I packed up my tools of the trade.

I grabbed Hank, shouldered my pack and out the door we went. We meandered around for a few minutes letting Phillip check us out. I made sure I was his perfect type, something he couldn't resist.

I was able to catch a glimpse of him checking me out in the reflection of the window. "Alright Hank we've got his attention, let's put our plan into effect," I said and off we went.

Hank and I just kept walking at one-point Phillip tried to do what he likes to do but I out ran him. When I got to the top of a rise, I stopped, turned, smiled and waved at him. That did it; he was mine and would have followed me to Hell.

He followed me all the way to the grove of trees. I didn't want him to see his grave so I had found enough debris to cover it up but not enough to fill it up. He was standing overlooking his grave never seeing it but I wasn't ready for him yet, but I could see he was ready for me.

As soon as I had my rain gear on I crept up behind him and said, "Hello Phillip." He nearly jumped off the ground and whirled around, as he did so I pushed him.

He fell backwards into the grave. "What the hell are you doin'?" he demanded.

"I'm doin' to you what you've done to these women and girls," I said and threw the pictures at him.

"I didn't do this, I was cleared!" he said indignantly.

"Tsk, tsk, tsk. Oh Phillip, why do you lie to me, but no matter, I'm your judge, jury and executioner and I find you guilty," I said as I pulled up my mask and pulled my goggles down.

"What do you mean? What are you doin'?" he stammered as he tried to escape.

Before he could scream for help I cut his throat and was sprayed with blood. I'm so glad I was able to get his medical records so I knew I wasn't going to get any diseases from his blood. I'll definitely get or try to get one of those masks that are one piece and can flip up or down. This is the last time I'll take hot blood on the little bit of exposed skin on my face.

"That's what I'm gonna do," I said to Phillip. I watched him slump down and the life left his eyes.

The bottom of the grave was covered with blood and was mixing with the dirt turning it into a red mud that seemed to be flowing as if lava. So when I started to throw the dirt over the body little droplets of blood and some globs of bloody dirt would fly up out of the hole. It actually took me longer to fill the hole than I thought it would. "Good lord Hank I didn't think I'd ever get this hole filled up!" I exclaimed and pulled some brush and limbs over the hole.

I pulled off my mask, goggles and rain suit; I shoved them in a bag and shoved that in my pack. "Well Hank, another one off the list. Come on let's see who's next," I said, looked around to make sure no one was around. Once I was sure the coast was clear, I shouldered my pack, took Hank's leash and started down the path singing a happy song.

CHAPTER TWELVE
HUNTING FOR ANSWERS

Hank and I checked out of our cabin early the next morning in search of our next pervert who escaped justice. The nearest one was very far down my list and it was a woman and she wasn't a pervert. She had been drunk when she hit a little boy on a bike. It was a remote area and she was a very clever woman. After she hit the boy and killed him she backed up and made it look as if she tried to miss him. She ran her car into a ditch and waited for someone to come along. By the time she was spotted and the police got there to administer a field sobriety test she had sobered up. Of course she passed the test with flying colors.

The police questioned everybody who was at the wedding and they all said she was smashed. They were ready to take her home but couldn't find her and since she just bought a new car they didn't even realize she was driving they assumed she had gotten a ride. Because she didn't have a criminal record and because she passed the test the police administered, it was considered a tragic accident. She was released without anything happening to her, she didn't even get a fine. Needless to say the community was up in arms.

Or I could go up into West Virginia and hunt down another woman who had killed her husband. She at least got probation even if it was only three months. She said it was an accident, a terrible accident. She didn't see her husband bending over in the driveway picking up a quarter. So she backed over him and then to get off of him she drove back over him. What the police didn't know was that she glued the quarter to the driveway ensuring her husband wouldn't be paying any attention to his surroundings.

"Hank I'm gonna have to do some thinkin' on this. Let's stop and get us a bite to eat. Hopefully I'll be able to figure it out," I said.

"Well Hank we're gonna head to Harpseville, West Virginia and hopefully I'll be able to find Mary Hollamar," I said and off we went to find number five on my list.

I walked off from James and his bimbo. I don't know why this bothered me so much but I was steaming. Well heck yeah I know what it is; I have a huge crush on him. When you're my height I don't find men tall enough to make me feel safe and he makes me feel safe.

I found Gerald and Sarah; we also found the last two bookstores of this day. "Are we gonna get our picnic fixings?" I asked like a little kid, then grabbed my throat and dropped to my knees.

"Bloody hell, not again," Gerald snapped and ran to the car.

Sarah had a couple of tissues which she shoved around my hand to catch the blood which was dripping but I had no wound. Gerald came back with some more and soon we had quite a little pile of them. "Parker my dear are you able to get up?" Sarah asked tenderly.

"I just need to sit a minute. These attacks are gettin' a bit much. As far as I'm concerned if I'm gonna feel the pain I should be able to see what's goin' on," I said and the blood finally stopped.

I got up and made sure my neck wasn't leaking any more. I looked around and thank god there wasn't anyone around. I can't stand being watched. "I'm alright now. I'm sorry I've upset you guys. I know it's upsetting and I'm very sorry to put you through this," I said and my stomach let out a great, loud gurgle.

"Parker we'll take you home and I'll fix you a meal fit for a queen," Sarah said.

"I was hopin' we could still have the picnic. I'm okay, really I am. I just need to be outside for a while," I said.

Gerald and Sarah just smiled at me. "Oh alright we'll have our picnic. There's a little market just up ahead and we'll be able to stock up on our picnic items," Sarah said.

"How did your search go?" Gerald asked.

"Pretty good. I got two books and found some information in the library. I also met a man named James Stuart at the first bookstore. His uncle said he would be able to help me," I said.

"Well where is he, we've heard so much about him," Sarah said.

"Well I left him outside the library swapping spit with some blonde slut," I said, shook my head and started to laugh.

Gerald had a wry smile on his face and Sarah was blushing. "What's the matter?" I asked.

"What you just told us doesn't surprise us. He's known around this area as a real ladies man. He always has a new woman on his arm," Gerald said.

"He's known for bein' extremely generous with his lady friends but it never lasts; six months is the longest any of his relationships last. I don't know why he's a good-looking man and very generous," Sarah said.

"Maybe the women push too hard and chase him away," Gerald said.

"Or maybe he just hasn't found Miss Right," Sarah said.

"Well it also might have something to do with the type of women he hangs out with," I said and shuddered.

"Parker what's the matter?" Sarah and Gerald asked in unison.

"Two more have been added to the list of Gracie's victims. The only problem with this is I can't see Gracie or what or where she's goin'. It's imperative that I find that book or there will be no stoppin' her. Oh crud," I said and fell silent.

Harpseville, West Virginia not too big, not too little, hopefully I won't stand out like a sore thumb. I drove around the town and caused such a stir. People actually came out of their businesses, stood on the sidewalks with their arms crossed and they just stared at me. I don't know what's going on but if all of this unwanted attention continues I'm going to have to call this operation off.

I went into one motel after another, all of them supposedly full, they weren't. I went in to the last motel in town, matter of fact not only was it the last motel I went to, it was just in the town limits.

"Can I help you?" the clerk asked.

"Yeah, can I get a room?" I asked waiting for the negative answer.

"Sure, we have plenty of rooms. Most folks don't come out this far," the clerk said.

"Well I've been to all the others and none of them would give me a room. They all said they were full even though there wasn't a car in the lot. How come they won't give me a room?" I asked.

"Because these idiots are still reeling from all the people that came here because of Mary Hollamar," the clerk said.

"Who?" I asked.

"She was the one that backed over her husband and then drove over him because she said she had to get the car off of him. We had so many reporters in town shoving microphones in our faces it made it near impossible to go out on the street," the clerk said.

"I remember hearin' about that. I just didn't think it happened here. What happened to her? Does she still live here?" I asked.

"She got off with a slap on the wrist. She moved probably three to four months ago," the clerk said.

"Do you know where she went? Did anybody warn the people of her new town?" I asked.

"We haven't got a clue. She packed up in the middle of the night and no one has seen her since. How long will you be stayin'?" the clerk asked.

"Just tonight. Could I get a king size bed and no smoking," I replied.

"Not a problem," the clerk said and handed me the key.

Once inside the room I threw my suitcase and pack on the bed. "Damn, well Hank we'll have to find another person to bring justice to," I said and pulled out my list.

"Parker you really have to tell your parents," Sarah said. This wasn't the first time we've had this conversation but it was going to be the last.

"I know and I'm gonna when we get home. I didn't want to worry them with just speculation on my part. But now that I'm feelin' their pain and bleedin' I have to tell them," I said.

"How about telling the police?" Gerald asked.

"No I don't do that anymore. I've done that in the past and all I got was laughed at. One time they brought me in as a suspect, my good god it took almost a month to get my name cleared! Since that little fiasco the police have to come to me. But even if they did come to me all I could tell them would be the names of the victims, even that might be wrong."

"When Abbigail Gustavian and Phillip Roscoe were finally able to come to me they showed me two different people. I can only assume that Marsh under Gracie's influence stole some of the costumes from Aunt Addie's attic. Since I'm bein' prevented from seein' I can only tell them it's Marsh and if it isn't; then the true killer would be free to kill again," I said and sighed a huge sigh.

"Well that does sound like a very big problem and could seriously cause problems with the investigation farther down the road. Let's put our heads together and try to solve this dilemma while we eat," Gerald said.

"You won't get any argument from me," I said and tried to laugh but Marsh was on my mind. All I could think of was the trouble Gracie was heading Marsh into. I really have to find the White Book and study it so I can defeat Gracie. I pray Marsh can find the strength to fight. I've been contacting her and on a couple of occasions I've seen her, she's a prisoner locked away in a cell.

We stopped at a beautiful park and walked to a covered area surrounded by beautiful flowering shrubs of purple, pink, and white. "Let's eat here. This is one of my favorite spots. Gerald proposed to me here," Sarah said and they looked at each other as if they were still newlyweds. I only hope and pray I find a love like this one day.

We had a feast fit for a king! "Sarah you out did yourself!" Gerald said.

"I second that. I hate to change the subject but I just had a thought. I could have Mom and Dad send me any information regarding any missing person cases. Hopefully I could find a pattern and that could possibly lead me to Marsh. Lord knows nothin' else I've tried has given me any results," I said.

"Well that sounds like a very good idea. Maybe if the authorities would contact you, you could see what they have. Then you could come up with an idea of where she's at. I'm surprised they haven't tried to reach you," Gerald said.

"I'm sure the police haven't a clue. If they're killed in different jurisdictions they'll never put it together. But when they do figure it out they can contact you for help. That way they won't think you're a crack pot or that you did it. I still can't understand that one," Sarah said.

"Well I figure that since they couldn't find the real killer and I knew all about the case, well they figured I must have done it. That's why they must come to me and if they don't, as hard as it is, I won't go to them," I said.

We were packing up when James walked up to us and I thought Sarah was going to faint and even Gerald was impressed with his size.

"James I'd like you to meet Gerald and Sarah Cosgrove. Gerald, Sarah this is James Stuart," I said.

"Very nice to meet you," they all said.

"Parker where did you run off to?" James asked.

"Well I wanted to give you and Bambi some privacy. Besides that I didn't need to see any more of her cheeks. But I'm sure those boys got a few visual aids," I said.

He gave me a rakish smile and said, "We're just friends and I haven't seen her in a while. The reason I'm here is because Uncle Robert has come up with a list of stores that might be of help to you," James said as he handed me a piece of paper.

I opened it up and there were ten names and addresses on it, some as far away as Italy. "Wow! Thank you very much and thank your uncle for me. Boy I'm gonna have a lot of traveling to do," I said and looked at the list again and handed it to Gerald and Sarah.

"Bloody hell this is a large list. Sarah and I can help you with the first four but the rest," Gerald said and stopped.

"Well if you'd let me I'd be glad to help you," James said.

I looked at James and then at Gerald and Sarah. Gerald shrugged but Sarah smiled and nodded her head giving me her approval. "Alright I accept your offer. Thank you very much," I said.

"Uncle Robert's number is on the bottom of the paper. When you're ready just give him a call and he'll let me know," James said, shook our hands and left.

I couldn't sit still so I decided to go out for a little drive. I drove around and I'm telling you Harpseville is a very nice little town. It was too bad that a killer had stained its good name.

I pulled into the parking lot of a mom and pop grocery store. "Now Hank I've got to go in and you've got to stay here. Now you be good and I'll be back shortly," I said.

I was in the store getting some supplies and just looking around. I was standing at the deli waiting for my turn when the people in front of me started taking about Mary Hollamar. One of the women was related to her and though she killed her husband, she still kept in touch with her.

She also said that since she'd moved to Slipsville she felt much better about herself and her life was so much better. I finally got my order; I left and got back to Hank. "Well Hank we're goin' to Slipsville after we eat," I said.

Hank and I left our room at 5:15 p.m. and were there in forty-five minutes. I found a phone booth with an intact phone book. What was even more surprising was the fact that Mary Hollamar was listed, I almost fell over!

I wrote down the address and found it very easily. She lived on the edge of town. I walked up to the door and knocked. A mid-sized woman answered the door and I knew it was her from the picture that I had. "I'm sorry to bother you but I am so lost and turned around and almost out of gas. I was wondering if you could help me?" I asked sweetly.

She looked at me and I guess she thought I was harmless so she opened the door. "Come on in. Let me get you a glass of water or something," Mary said.

"Thank you very much. My name is Abby," I said and stuck out my hand.

"Well you're more than welcome my name is Mary," and she stuck out her hand which I took and shook.

"You know Mary your house is just lovely. I'm sure your husband and kids are so proud of it and you," I said sweetly and smiled.

"Well thank you but I don't have a family; they're too much work and trouble. Let me get you a glass of water, I'll give you directions and then you'll have to go," Mary said.

"Sure, not a problem. I'm sorry if I offended you," I said and I watched her go into the kitchen.

I quietly followed her into the kitchen and silently pulled my knife from my purse. "Mary the water won't be necessary," I said and slid my knife across her throat cutting deeply into her flesh severing her arteries.

The blood sprayed the window and the wall over the sink. She tried to turn but I wasn't about to let her. I sure didn't want to get sprayed. She finally dropped to the floor. Once she was dead I went through the house wiping off anything I might have touched. Once I was sure it was clean I walked out the front door using my towel to remove all trace of my presence.

When I got to the Jeep I crossed her name off my list. "Come on Hank let's go back to our room and tomorrow we'll be off for greener pastures," I said and kissed the top of Hank's head.

CHAPTER THIRTEEN
PREDATOR BECOMES PREY

When we got back to the motel I got cleaned up, grabbed my list and sat down on the bed. Hank jumped up next to me and looked as if he were studying it. I finally decided I was going to go after that drunken floozy who hopefully still lives in Tennessee. "Hankie my love, we're off early tomorrow to look for Katherine Gargard. I'm hopin' she still lives in Misty Field. If she doesn't the next best thing would be she left a forwarding address, so let's turn in and get some rest," I said and Hank gave a small woof of approval.

We left early the next morning and the pop I bought at the store shot straight through me. I saw the sign for Robberson's Picnic Area so I slowed down. The parking lot was empty, there wasn't anyone in the area surrounding the parking lot so I pulled in. The parking lot was gravel so I crunched through the parking lot and stopped directly stopped in front of the bathrooms.

By the time I stopped, I thought I was going to explode. I had to go to the bathroom so bad I didn't think I'd make it to the toilet. I gave a quick check and didn't see anything; it was empty except for me so I ran to a stall.

I stood up and pulled up my pants, I was trying to get out as soon as possible. I wasn't in super panic mode because there wasn't any crunching. So when the door to the stall burst open to say I was stunned was an understatement. The door hit me so hard it knocked me backwards into the wall where I cracked my head hard enough to stun me. I was grabbed and dragged outside by my hair. There were four of them; they passed from one to another slapping and punching me.

I pulled away; one of them tripped me and down I went and I was kicked several times hard in my ribs. I was bloody and bruised but I somehow managed to get away from them and raced to my Jeep. I pulled the door open and got to the pistol that Grandfather got for me years ago, when I opened the door Hank jumped out!

For not being a very large guy he sure could pack a punch. He speared one of my attackers in his chest and wouldn't let go! I pulled out my pistol and shot the first man right between the eyes. There wasn't anyone around to see what I was going to do to these idiots.

I shot the second one in the throat and down he went. The third one in the chest and the one Hank held in the left eye. Even with all the noise from the gunshots it didn't bother Hank at all.

Once things had calmed down then and only then was I able to get Hank back to the Jeep. While I was there I had to fight off a wave of nausea as soon as that passed I pulled out my knife.

I walked up to the one I shot in the chest and squatted down next to him. "You messed with the wrong person. I saved you for last because I wanted you to see your friends die first. Now we're gonna have some fun." I made sure he suffered greatly before I finally released him from his pain. As soon as that was done I went back into the bathroom and wiped everything down. When I came back out I decided I'd drag the bodies behind the bathroom and hide them in the bushes.

When I drug the first body behind the bathroom and started to hide him in the bushes, I noticed there was a drop off which ended in a deep dark ravine. "Well scumbag no one will find you for a long time or forever," I said and pushed him over the edge. I did this three more times, when this was done, I made sure no one would be able to tell I was back here.

I looked around, since there still wasn't any traffic I was able to pick up the shell casings without having to rush around. When I was satisfied that I had cleaned everything up I started looking around for their vehicle. It wasn't in the parking lot or anywhere on the road. I walked back to my Jeep and opened the door. "Hank where in the heck did they park?" I asked and then for the first time I noticed the barn across the road.

"Well Hank I wonder if they put it in the barn? Well there's only one way to find out let's take a little walk," I said and I took Hank out of the Jeep and walked to the barn.

We walked across the street and went up to the barn and an old cement driveway. There was a lock on it, a new lock, now this was interesting. "Hank why would this be locked?" I asked.

I walked closer and peeked inside, not touching anything. "Well what do you know, no wonder I didn't hear them. I wonder if they've done this before. Well no matter, they won't hurt anyone again," I said and walked back to the Jeep.

"Come on Hank, let's get out of here," I said and we left the area and carnage behind us.

I called home and just before Mom answered the phone I got hit with several flashes. Sarah grabbed the phone from me and yelled for Gerald. "Mrs. MacStuart this is Sarah. No nothing is wrong with Parker. She's having a vision. I'm sure there is nothing wrong. Here she is," Sarah said.

"No Mom I'm fine, really I am. I have something to tell you, it's about Marsh. Gracie has her and she has killed many times. I just got a flash of the woman she killed in West Virginia and then she was attacked at a picnic area and killed all of them," and Mom started to cry.

As soon as she was done crying, boy did I get my head chewed off for not telling her sooner. I apologized about a thousand times. Mom also apologized the same amount of times because she finally figured out why I didn't tell her sooner.

I asked Mom if there had been any news stories about any missing people maybe with a criminal past. She told me there had been several and they were all let off on technicalities. "That's got to be Marsh, or I should say Gracie, but I can't prove it. She's usin' disguises and no two have shown me the same person."

"Mom I've got to go. Sarah is takin' me to several bookstores today and hopefully I can find what I need to get these things to stop. Mom tell Dad and the quads I love them. Mom I love you and if you see Marsh, stay away from her and call the police. Promise me Mom promise me that none of you will see her!" I pleaded.

"I promise Parker. I'll make sure everyone knows. Be careful my baby girl. I love you so very much," Mom said and we hung up.

Sarah and I were gone all day and by the end of the day I felt as if I had traveled 50,000 miles. It didn't make it any better because I came up with absolutely nothing. "Sarah I'm sorry for draggin' you all over the place and then not findin' anything," I said disgustedly.

"Parker don't worry about it. If you continue the search tomorrow Gerald and I are busy. You know you could call and get in touch with James," she said and smiled.

I just looked at her, "You've got to be kiddin' me. Do you like him? What do you think of him?" I asked.

"Yes I do like him even though I don't know him. Despite all the women he has supposedly had, I really think he is a decent man. I also think he likes you as well as respects you. I can see it in his eyes when he looks at you."

"I also think that if you give him a chance he will become a very good friend and would protect you from any and all danger, real or imagined. So my dear Parker give that very large man a chance," Sarah said.

"Well if you think he's a good man, what does Gerald think of him?" I asked.

"If you mean James Stuart I think he is an honorable man even though he likes to chase the ladies. You could do way worse; he will definitely protect you against whatever would come your way. So call the uncle and then have James take you and find this book so you can free Miss Marsha," Gerald said.

"Oh alright I'll call his uncle. Hello Mr. Stuart, this is Parker MacStuart. James said if I needed his help I should call you and you'd get in touch with him," I said and felt extremely stupid.

"Well Miss MacStuart you are in luck. Jimmy is right here. Let me get him," he said and laid the phone down.

In the distance I could hear him call, "Jimmy, Jimmy boy, the wee lass, Miss MacStuart is on the line." I started to laugh, I never figured that someone as big as James would be called Jimmy. And I never in a million years thought I'd ever be called a wee lass.

"Hello Parker, how can I help you?" James asked in that deep bass voice of his.

"There are some bookstores that are out of the country and I was wondering if you could help me find some of them?" I asked.

"When do you want to go?" James asked.

"Well if it's possible I'd like to go tomorrow," I said and waited for him to say he couldn't go.

"Tomorrow is fine. May I make a suggestion?" he asked.

"Sure, go ahead," I replied.

"Since this is an urgent situation my suggestion is to pack a bag and stay out until every one of the stores on the list has been visited," James said.

I was silent for a little bit and then I said, "I think that's a good idea. I just don't want you to think I'm loose and easy," I said.

"I would never think that. I know you are a woman of virtue. I'll pick you up at six in the morning if that's alright with you," James said.

"Yes that's fine and thank you. See you tomorrow," I said and hung up. Then a thought hit me, how did he know I was a woman of virtue? Do I have a look that his usual women don't? Oh well I'm not going to worry about it and I shrugged.

"Sarah, I'm leavin' tomorrow and I'll be gone for oh I don't know, I guess a couple of days," I said.

"I'll get your bag for you. I'll fix you and James something you can take with you, so if you'll excuse me I've got some work to do," Sarah said happily and took off.

"Thank you," I called to her back.

I kept checking my rearview mirror to see if the police were after me. I sure felt better when I left West Virginia behind and I entered Kentucky.

For the next hour I kept checking my rearview mirror and finally an hour and a half after the attack, I knew I was safe. "Well Hank we're safe," I said and felt much better, then I noticed the scrape and bruise on my left cheek.

"Oh great Hank, how am I gonna explain this?" I asked, sighed then turned on the radio. I keep flipping through the stations; there was absolutely nothing about the attack.

As the day went on the cloudier it became and at 2:00 p.m. it started to rain and rain fairly hard. It was raining so hard that at 3:00 p.m. I pulled into Crawlins. I pulled into the parking lot of a small motel and parked underneath the covered area next to the entrance. I checked my face," Well Hank here goes nothin'," I said and put on one of my floppy hats and pulled it down so my bruised, scraped side of my face was hidden.

I didn't have any problems whatsoever, I got us a nice room and all parking spaces were covered. I just pulled in my parking space, we got in our room when the hail started. It hailed for almost an hour, nothing very large but it would damage vehicles out in the open and vegetation. Once the hail ended the rain started again and the flooding began.

I was in the motel for three days and there was flooding throughout the states of Kentucky, West Virginia, Virginia, Tennessee, parts of Ohio and Indiana. The networks were showing the devastation and one of the pictures was of the picnic area where I was attacked.

The entire area had been scoured away and all evidence of my crime had been washed away. "Well Hank I worried about this for nothin', now let's get on the road. Misty Field, Tennessee here we come," I said and I packed up the Jeep.

Since we left late in the day we only traveled a few hours and a couple hundred miles and then I stopped for the night. We left early the next morning and arrived mid-morning in Misty Field. I found a very nice bed and breakfast; since the bed and breakfast was so nice I decided to stay a week.

I also wanted to replenish my funds; I just wanted to replace the money I had spent on my Jeep, food, motels and gas before I head out west where there might be less of my banks. I was very lucky that there were two of them here in town. Once I was settled I went to my bank and withdrew $15,000 without a problem. They were very kind and courteous to me.

I was in such shock about not having to fight to cash my check I completely forgot to ask for some smaller bills. But not to worry another of my banks was across the street. I pulled open the door and lo and behold there stood Katherine Gargard. "Can I help you?" Katherine asked.

"Yes I need to cash this and I'd like some of it in twenties," I said and she looked at me as if I were a criminal. It also seemed as if she wanted me to tell her why I wanted the money and I wasn't going to.

"Why do you need so much money?" she asked.

"I really don't think that's any of your business," I said.

"Well miss you aren't one of our regular customers. I know who they are and how much money they have," Katherine said.

"Well Katherine why I need money and how much money I have is none of your business. My check and my I.D. is all you should care about. I know you'll need to get authorization to cash this, so just contact whoever it is you need to," I said hotly.

She went and got her manager and he came over, oh this ought to be good. "How can I help you miss?"

"I just want to cash this check and get some of the money in smaller bills. And all I got was lip from her," I said hotly.

"I'm sorry Miss but we've had some people passin' forged checks," the manager said.

"Well I have my I.D. and if you need to call my branch back home I even have their phone number along with the name and extension of the manager," I said and handed him my check.

The manager looked at the check and said, "Come this way Miss Larkwood," and we walked to his desk. Twenty minutes later I had my cash, all in hundreds but I was so annoyed and angry I wasn't going to ask anyone for smaller bills, so back to the first bank I went.

I walked back to the first bank and as soon as I stepped through the door I was met by the manager. "Miss Larkwood is there a problem?" he asked and truly meant it.

"Well I went over to my other bank to take care of some business and I wanted to exchange some of the bigger bills you gave me. Well a certain person treated me as if I were a criminal. I got so upset I forgot to ask them to exchange them. So can you do that for me?" I asked almost on the verge of tears.

"I'm sorry you had to go through such a hassle over there," and he nodded toward the other bank and then he continued, "I've heard many stories about the service and I know exactly who you're talking about. Please excuse me while I take care of this for you," he said.

He was only gone for a few minutes and when he returned I had $5,000 in smaller bills. "Thank you very, very much Mr. Linwood, I really do appreciate it," I said.

"You're very welcome Miss Larkwood. Anything you need don't hesitate to ask," Mr. Linwood said and shook my hand.

I walked out of the bank, went to the diner and there sat Katherine, she seemed to be putting something suspicious in her coffee.

She saw me, walked over to me and sat down. "You know I can change those bills for you for a fee," Katherine said.

"What are you talkin' about?" I asked.

"I can change those counterfeit bills for you for a fee," Katherine said again.

"What? What did you say? How dare you! Get out of here," I said hotly.

"Well I'm sorry you feel that way," Katherine said as she stood up and continued, "Don't take this woman's money, it's counterfeit."

After that little crack I stood up; all heads turned toward me. "There's nothin' wrong with my money. If you don't believe me call Mr. Linwood. Besides that are you gonna take the word of a drunken thief over Mr. Linwood?" I looked directly at Katherine. I almost said murderer but I didn't want anybody to know I knew about her.

"Katherine just go. You've caused enough trouble in this town. Miss you and your money are welcome here. Now Katherine get out," the owner of the diner said.

Katherine threw her cup at the owner and stormed out. "Dirty drunken bitch," one of the customers said and continued, "Lou I've got to go."

"Alright see you Frank," Lou the owner said and he started to clean up the broken cup.

"Come on Miss; sit down here at the bar. Don't pay any attention to her, none of us do. When she gets a little under her belt, well she gets nasty."

"I'm sorry I shouldn't have said that about her, but I'm not passin' counterfeit money. That was a lie and it made me angry, so I apologize. By the way my name is Bede," I said and stuck out my hand.

"Well Bede my name is Lou and don't worry about it. You're not the first nor will you be the last to have a run in with her. We had a real dozy in here last week. Frank's wife Sue said if she ever insulted her again she'd kill her and then she slapped Katherine across the face," Lou said.

"Oh that's not good," I said sympathetically and if anybody suspected me I could throw this name out.

Sure enough James was at the house before six. "Good morning," Sarah said and opened the door.

"Good morning Mrs. Cosgrove," James said.

"Good morning James," I said as I went running by them like a fool. All he had time to do was give a quick wave.

"Has she been doin' this very long?" James asked.

"She's been up since three and she's been running around like this since four. If she would sit down for five minutes she'd pass out," Sarah said.

I came running by again, "Sarah I can't find my camera!" I yelled.

"It's in your bag Parker. You packed it last night. I was there with you. You just need to take a deep breath and relax," Sarah said calmly.

"Relax, I don't know what that means," I said and went to run by them again but James grabbed me.

"Parker look at me," James said and I did.

"Relax, you're fine. Sarah's fine, Gerald's fine and I'm fine. Everything will turn out. I'm here to help you. If you don't have everything we'll buy it. Now let's go," James said.

"You're right. I'm sorry. I'm bein' stupid. I'm actually bein' a stupid, weak woman which I try not to be," I said.

"There's no need to apologize, you're not weak and we all know it. Now let's get going. Good bye Sarah, I'll take very good care of her," James said.

"I know you will. Parker be careful," Sarah said and hugged me.

"I will Sarah. Thank you and Gerald very much," I said and squeezed back.

Once in the car James said to me, "You're very lucky to have people who care about you. Are your parents still alive?" James asked.

"Oh yeah, they're back home. I'm here because I inherited Briargate and I was goin' through the paperwork and cataloging everything here. Then this thing with Marsh started," I said and fell silent.

"Parker, I am sorry. You have my word that I'll do everything in my power to help you and protect you," James said.

"But why do you care so much about me and what's goin' on?" I asked.

He just shrugged and I didn't think he was going to say anything but he did. "Because I like you," and he smiled at me.

I looked at him and smiled. "Oh brother," I said and we both started laughing.

We made it to the ferry and settled down for the crossing to France. It was a beautiful day so we enjoyed our breakfast as we watched the water and the waves from the ferry.

We landed in France and we were headed to the first name on the list and it was Keffenach. It was a small city or I should say town with a population of 10,353 and was in the Alsace region.

We checked out the bookstore and all the rest on the list in France and found absolutely nothing. We traveled the length and breadth of Italy; checking every bookstore on the list and then some. But there was nothing, nothing at all. The only thing we found were stares from the locals.

James dropped me off; he actually walked me to the door. "James I truly appreciate your being with me, thanks very much," I said.

"Parker it was my pleasure. Any time you need me I'm here for you. Once I check in with Uncle Robert and see if he has anything else, I'll give you a buzz," James said and the door opened.

"Thanks James, talk to you later," I said and watched him walk back to his car and take off.

While I was in town I did all the tourist things and I swear every time I turned around Katherine was close at hand. I think she's stalking me; this could really work in my favor. I could kill her and claim it was self-defense.

I walked into the diner and there stood Lou. He was a very nice man and I really liked him. He was the first man I have ever felt this way about and I think he feels the same way about me. I know he's a lot older than I am but oh he's so nice. "Lou is there a back way out of here. That crazy Katherine won't leave me alone!" I said excitedly.

"Okay, slow down, come this way. Go out the door and up the stairs. Here's the keys to my place. My grandparents live there, I take care of them. Just tell them you're a friend and Katherine's botherin' you, they'll understand," Lou said and he slapped the keys in my hands.

I went upstairs, unlocked the door and stepped inside, "Hello, any one home? My name is Bede and Lou sent me up here," I called out.

Out stepped a tall thin older woman with beautiful silver hair that curled ever so slightly on her neck. She was dressed in black pants and a lavender blouse; she was stunning. "I'm sorry I was in the front room in the closet puttin' up some coats. Who did you say you were?" she asked.

"My name is Bede. Lou sent me up here because Katherine won't leave me alone," I said.

"Well if Lou sent you up here then you're just fine. My name is Maria and this is my husband Al," she said. He was a very distinguished gentlemen; Lou was the spitting image of him. Al was tall and balding, he was dressed in black pants, white shirt and a red cardigan.

"Very nice to meet you," I said and I shook their hands.

"Bede come sit, have some cakes, some milk and coffee," Al said.

"Well thank you very much, I'd love some," I said.

Once seated the topic of conversation turned to Katherine. "Lou tells us you had a run in with Katherine," Maria said.

"Yeah I did. She came up to me and accused me of bein' a counterfeiter. So I said some nasty things back to her and since then wherever I go she seems to be there," I said.

"She has been known to do that, she's a very unpleasant young woman," Al said.

"That's for sure and when she drinks it gets even worse," Maria said.

"She gets away with this behavior because she knows dirty little secrets about people here in Misty Field, many of them have connections. One of these days she's gonna say or do something to the wrong person and they're gonna hurt her," Al said.

"Boy she sounds like a real witch," I said.

"She is and since you did what you did she will definitely come after you," Al said.

"Bede I don't want you to think I'm rude but I think for your own safety you should leave town," Maria said.

"You mean she would actually try to hurt me?" I asked incredulously.

"Yes she would. She has hurt other people on other occasions. The little boy she ran over was her ex-lover's child," Al said.

"I didn't know she knew who it was? I thought it was a remote area, not very well traveled. So why did she do it?" I asked.

"Yes it is a little traveled road. She was at a wedding and did what she always does and that is drink too much. Dob, her ex-lover well his wife, Sissy found out about the affair. Sissy told him to stop or she'd leave him and take Paul so far away he'd never find them," Maria said.

"So he told Katherine the affair was over and two months later Paul was dead. Coincidence, I don't think so. Katherine had been to that house and knew that boy would ride his bike on that road. It was murder plain and simple," Al said.

"She is truly an evil woman," I said and for a minute I felt very light and thought about my friend and sister Parker.

"Excuse me Bede," Maria said and went to answer the phone.

When she came back she said, "Lou says the coast is clear. But to be on the safe side he's gonna make sure you get an escort home."

"Thank you very much for everything, I truly appreciate it. It was very nice meeting both of you," I said.

"The pleasure was all ours. You are always welcome here Bede," Maria said as we shook hands and then I went down to the diner.

"Ah Bede, this is my daughter Clarice. She's gonna take you back to your room. Katherine doesn't know what she drives, so she'll be able to get you and Hank back without any problems," Lou said.

"Lou, I want to thank you very much," I said and continued, "Hi Clarice."

"Hi Bede, come on I'll take you home. See yah later Pop," Clarice said.

She drove me and Hank back to the bed and breakfast; she even walked with me to my room. "Well Bede I'll see you later. Pop would love you to stop by later but he won't ask you yet, he's kinda shy, but I'm not," Clarice said and smiled.

"You're kiddin'. You know, this will sound crazy, but I'm so glad because I have a huge crush on him. Maybe I'll stop by later. Thanks Clarice," I said and closed the door behind her.

I took Hank out at nine and since the diner was open I stopped by. Sure enough Katherine was in her car watching me. I stayed at the diner for an hour and then made my way back to my room. I made sure Katherine saw me go back to my room. I went to the window and looked out knowing she would see me. I left the window up just an inch or two and at midnight I heard the window start to rise up. In the shadows of the room the figure of Katherine appeared.

"Hello Katherine," I said.

She rushed me and I saw the glint of light off the blade of her knife. She cut me again and again. "Help! Help me!" I screamed and punched her in the face.

"Bede, Bede! Open the door!" the manager screamed.

"I can't! Help! Katherine's in here, she's cut me! Help me!" I screamed again and hit her again.

"Well Katherine let's see how you like it," I said. I grabbed the knife from her and started to slice her.

Before I could slice her some more, just to play with her, but the door started to splinter and I could see the light from the hallway.

"Help!" I screamed and then I whispered, "Good bye Katherine," and I plunged the knife into her neck.

The owner of the bed and breakfast was the first one in then the police were next. "Come on Bede let's get you out of here and to the hospital," the owner said.

They took me to the hospital and stitched me up, the police questioned me and I gave my statement. Katherine was pronounced dead at the scene, when I went to the inquest it was found that I acted in self-defense and no charges would be filed.

Two days after the inquest I left town with a heavy heart. I was leaving Lou and that hurt. I sobbed for over an hour but found I just could not turn the car around. I drove all day and into the evening, I finally had to stop for the night because I was exhausted. I decided I was going to stay a couple of days to rest up and let my wounds heal. I was going to head west where the story of my brush with death would be unknown.

CHAPTER FOURTEEN
RESCUED!

As I was sitting in yet another motel room, I started to cry. I realized that I was alone, I had been released from the prison she held me in guarded by a faceless male spirit. Plus I had done some very bad things while Gracie was in control. For some reason Gracie was gone, so was the faceless male spirit and the knowledge of what she did while in control was almost more than I could bear.

I threw myself down on the bed and just started screaming into the pillow and pounding the mattress. I rolled over on my back and looked up at the ceiling. The tears were rolling down my face and into my ears. I closed my eyes and called out for Parker. "Parker, please help me! Oh Parker please help me!" I cried some more and shut my eyes.

My mind wandered back to when Parker and I were small kids. We would play a game where she would read me and talk to the dead by pretending to use toy telephones. With these very pleasant memories on my mind I relaxed and smiled at those two little carefree girls. "Hello," Parker said.

"Parker! Help me! Please help me!" I screamed.

"Marsh! Where are you? Show me where you're at!" Parker yelled.

"I don't know! I don't know! Parker please help me! I've done some very bad things! Please help me!" I begged.

"Marsh, shh, try to relax. You didn't do this, it was Gracie. Don't you dare blame yourself and don't you do anything stupid to yourself. Now you try and relax and I'm gonna see if I can find you!" Parker yelled.

"Parker how come I'm alone?" I asked.

"Someone named Lou is prayin' for you. He's added his prayers to mine and he drove Gracie out. I found you, you're in Missouri. Marsh, Lou gave you a card, it's in your pocket. I want you to call him. Do you understand me, you call him! Talk to him; stay on the phone with him. Tell him you're in trouble; tell him you're runnin' from an abusive boyfriend, I don't care what you tell him, just stay on the phone with him!"

"He's driven Gracie out with his prayers. His feelings for you are very strong. Marsh please call him, please I beg you to call him because he'll help you if you let him!" Parker pleaded with me.

"Alright I'll call him, but will you come here to get me? Parker please come and help me! I'm begging you! Parker please help me!" I screamed.

Marsh I'll be there as soon as I can, I promise you I'll be there! I promise you; I'll be there! Marsh please call Lou!" Parker screamed and the connection was lost.

"Parker! Parker! Parker! Oh shoot dear god help me please! I don't want to do this anymore!" I screamed and fumbled to dial Lou's number.

"Lou! Lou! This is Bede, but that's not my real name! My name is Marsha! Please Lou I need help! Please help me!" I screamed.

"Oof," I gasped, I dropped my camera and sat down hard in the middle of the hallway.

"Sarah, Gerald! Do you know anyone that has a private jet that I could borrow or that would fly me to Missouri?" I asked.

"Why? Why do you need to go?" Sarah asked. If it would have been anyone other than Gerald and Sarah they would have had me committed to the loony bin.

"It was Marsh; she's wrestled control away from Gracie. There's a man named Lou, he's in love with her and he's prayin' for her. For some reason, his prayers are stronger than mine but in combination with mine they broke Gracie's hold. Crud true love, her true love broke Gracie's hold over Marsh! I've got to get there!" I yelled.

"I'm sorry I didn't mean to yell," then my eyes lit up and I continued, "I'm callin' James!"

"You know I think he has a pilot's license," Gerald said.

"Hello Mr. Stuart, this is Parker. I've got to speak to James! Please this is an emergency!" I shouted.

"Jimmy! Jimmy boy! It's the wee lass! Says it's an emergency!" Mr. Stuart shouted.

"Parker what's the matter?" James asked.

"I just talked to Marsh. There's a guy named Lou and he's prayin' for her and with his prayers mixed with mine, Marsh drove Gracie out for a while. I've got to get to Missouri! Do you know of anyone that has a private jet I could hire?" I yelled.

"Parker pack your bags I'll be there in half an hour," James said and hung up.

"Sarah, James is pickin' me up in half an hour! I've got to get packed!" I yelled and ran up the stairs.

"Marsh if you can still hear me, I'm comin'! I'm comin' my sister. Please god, please protect Marsh until I get there. Amen," I said and threw my clothes in my suitcase.

I sat up in bed and for a couple of minutes I had to think about where I was. I was so confused and to top it off I had the strangest dream. I dreamed Parker and I were on the phone playing the game we did when we were younger. She said that I had to call Lou and she would be here as soon as possible. I needed to relax and stay as calm as possible and don't leave my room.

Gracie was gone but for how long. It felt so good to be free of her but the memory of what she had done while in control sickened me and I started sobbing. I wanted to turn myself in but I WOULD wait for Parker, she'll know what to do. Besides that she said not to leave my room.

I picked up the phone and called Lou. "Hello?" Lou said.

"Lou this is Bede, please don't hang up. I need to talk to you. I need help, I'm in trouble. I lied to you; my name isn't Bede its Marsha Larkwood. I had to lie because I didn't want to be found. I can't tell you any more than that," I said and started crying.

"Bede or Marsha, it doesn't matter to me. Where are you? You know I'll do anything to help you. Please Marsha, just tell me where you are," Lou said and waited.

"Marsha? Marsha? Marsha are you there?" Lou asked.

"Lou please help me," then there was silence.

"Marsha?" Lou said.

"I'm sorry there's no one here by that name. This is Bede. Who's callin'?" I asked and for some reason Lou didn't answer.

I hung up and said, "Oh well Hank, wrong number. I'm goin' back to sleep."

"Parker, James is here," Sarah said as she stuck her head inside the room.

"Alright I'm ready. Sarah will you and Gerald be alright. Oh what am I sayin'. Could you tell Mr. Barlowe that I have some very urgent business at home? I don't know how long I'll be gone," I said as I grabbed my bag.

"Parker, we'll be fine, don't worry about us. You've got to save Miss Marsha. Is there anything you want us to do?" Sarah asked.

"How long has it been since you had a vacation?" I asked.

"It's been quite a long time," Sarah said.

"Why don't you take a vacation? You work so hard all the time. Sarah I want you to know I truly appreciate you and Gerald," I said and squeezed her.

"Parker thank you. If there's anything we can ever do for you don't hesitate to ask," Sarah said.

"Believe me Sarah if I need anything I'll get in touch with you. There's one thing I'd like you and Gerald to do, pray for Marsh. Pray for her several times a day," I said.

"That we will do Parker, we'll do it gladly," Sarah said and we were at the door and there stood James.

"Sarah here's the flight plan and all pertinent information. I'll take very good care of her. Come on now Parker, we've got to go," James said.

"Sarah I'll call you as soon as I get there," I said and hugged her and then I said, "Bye Sarah, tell Gerald I said good bye. I'll be back here as soon as I can."

"I will Parker, good bye," Sarah said and out the door we went.

I woke up the next morning and I wasn't feeling good at all. "Come on Hank let's go for a walk. It won't be a long one. I'm just not feelin' good at all. Matter of fact I haven't felt this nasty since Parker and I went for a walk and I got bit by a fly. I haven't seen any," I said. I pulled back the sheets, sure enough there was a big black fly in my bed.

We walked around to the back of the motel. "Oh look Hank at those lovely weeds. This is as far as we go. Please do your business." As Hank dutifully did what he was supposed to do I felt a wave of nausea come over me. I knew there was absolutely no way I was going to make it to the bathroom.

I threw up not once but twice and once done I felt as if I was going to die. "Hank let's go back to the room, I've got to go to bed," I said and staggered back to the room.

I just barely managed to get back to the room and I had to run full out for the bathroom. I threw up and it just kept coming up. I finally gave one last gag and that was it. I crawled out of the bathroom and went to the door. I put up the do not disturb sign, locked the door, fell on the bed, kicked off my shoes and curled up under the blankets. "Hank guard the room and please be a good boy," I said. I prayed I'd feel better after a nap but if this is like the last time, it won't do any good.

I woke up and I was freezing; I had sweat pouring off of me. I walked into the bathroom, well it was actually more like I staggered into the bathroom, stripped out of my clothes and took a hot shower.

Once that was done I put on my pajamas and went back to bed. Around 8:30 p.m. I woke up, still feeling miserable but Hank had to go out and of course it was raining. Once that was done I fed Hank, I took a drink of water and crawled back into bed.

"Parker! Parker! Can you hear me? Parker where are you? Parker can you hear me? Please help me, I'm so sick," I cried.

"Marsh I can hear you. I'm sorry for the fly but I need you to stay where you're at. You haven't left Jasperville have you?" Parker asked.

"No I'm still at the A-1 Motel. Parker please hurry. I'm really sick," I said.

"Marsh I have to talk to Lou. What's his last name?" Parker asked.

"His last name is Spagtini, Louis Spagtini. He lives with his daughter and grandparents over the diner in Misty Field, Tennessee and I should never have left there or him," I cried out.

"Marsh he'll help you if you let him. I know he feels the same way about you. Be strong Marsh and you'll be able to go to him," Parker said.

I sucked in a deep breath of air. "Parker what's the matter?" James asked.

"It's Marsh, I made her very sick. Gracie wasn't in control but now I think she's back. Can I use my cell phone; it's not going to hurt anything is it?" I asked.

"No it'll be fine. Who are you callin' and how did you make her sick?" James asked.

"My Mom. I have to find something out. I made her sick by sending a big black fly to her. It bit her and she's allergic to its bite. I figured if she was sick she couldn't get on the road. But now I don't know," I said.

"Mom, Gracie is buried with the rest of her family, isn't she?" I asked.

"Well I'm pretty sure she's with the rest of the family. Why?" Mom asked.

"I need to be sure. I have to ask you to do something for me. It might be a little nasty but it has to be done. Could you please go and check to make sure Gracie's body is still in her grave. Could you also look up a phone number for me?" I asked.

"Parker it might take a little while but I'll make sure Gracie is where she's supposed to be. What name do you need me to look up?" Mom asked.

"The name is Louis Spagtini he's in Misty Field, Tennessee. I'll try to contact him but if I can't get through, I'll call him. Mom thanks, I'll call you back in a few," I said.

I closed my eyes and let my mind wander. "Louis, Louis Spagtini," I called and waited to see if I could get an answer or a glimmer.

"Louis, Louis," then I thought I'd try something else.

"Lou, Lou, Lou Spagtini. Open your mind to me," I said and I waited a little bit and then I saw the glimmer of light.

"Lou, Lou Spagtini. I know you can hear me. I won't hurt you. I'm a very good friend of Marsha Larkwood, you know her as Bede. I'm here to help her," I said and the glimmer became a blazing bon fire.

"Lou, Lou Spagtini?" I asked as I appeared to him in his room. He was tall about 6' 3" or 6' 4", balding with his hair cut very short, almost shaved, clean shaven and hairy, not as hairy as James seems to be, but hairy.

"I'm Lou, who are you?" he asked.

"My name is Parker MacStuart and I'm Marsh's very good friend, she's my sister. She's in terrible danger and trouble. You probably won't believe me but she's not in control of herself. She has been taken over by a vicious killer named Gracie."

"Your prayers, the prayers of her true love added to mine have broken the hold if only for a little bit. Keep prayin' for her and if she calls again keep her on the phone for as long as possible. When I find her will you come to her aid?" I asked.

"Yes I will, I'll gladly do whatever it takes to help her. I don't know her but I'm in love with her," Lou said.

"Now I must tell you one last thing before I go, do not go to her unless I tell you or unless I'm there with you," I said.

"But why can't I go to her?" Lou asked.

"Because if you go to her without me or without me tellin' you it's safe, you'll be in great danger and do much harm to Marsh. Promise me you won't go to her without me. Promise me or great harm will befall you and your family," I said urgently.

"I promise, I promise I won't do anything to hurt Marsha or my family. I'll wait here until you call me. I promise on my daughter's head," Lou said.

"Thank you Lou and Marsha will thank you when she's well," I said and disappeared.

"James I contacted Lou. We've got to go there first," I said.

"Alright Parker, do you want to get out of the plane now?" James asked.

"We landed?" I asked.

"Yeah twenty minutes ago," he said.

"Well what are we waitin' for? I'm gonna call my Mom. Mom what did you find out?" I asked.

"Parker I found the grave, she's there and here's the address and phone number. Anything else?"

"Not right now. If I need anything else I'll let you know. I've got to go, talk to you later. Love you," I said.

"Love you too Parker," Mom said.

"Parker where to now Missouri or to Lou?" James asked.

"Let's go to Lou, here's the address. I'm gonna call him, let him know we're comin' to see him," I said, off we sped and I made my call to Sarah and Gerald.

"Parker, Parker," I called weakly.

"Marsh I'm here. You're gonna be okay soon you just hang in there a little bit longer. I'm comin' as soon as I can. I promise you, I'll be there as soon as I can," Parker said.

"Oh Parker I'm so sick, please help me!" I cried.

"Marsh relax you're gonna be fine. I'll be there soon; you just take the medicine on the night stand and go to sleep. You'll feel better in a few days," parker said.

"What medicine? Where'd this come from? Parker did you do this? Thanks Parker, I can always count on you," I said and took the medicine.

Before I fell asleep I made sure Hank had food and water and that he got to go out and use the bathroom. "Hank I don't know if you can understand me, but can you please go to the bathroom in the bathroom if I can't get up? Please Hank can you do that for me?" I asked and fell into bed.

We pulled up in front of the diner four hours after we landed. I looked across the street and I noticed a pyramid of light and then the male faceless spirit stepped out of the shadows. "James look!" I exclaimed and pointed.

"Bloody hell, Parker let's take a look. Who is that faceless man?" James asked.

"So you saw him too. I have an idea but I won't say it yet. It might hurt Marsh," I said.

"Sounds good to me," James said.

We ran across the street and the store was still open. I just wasn't sure if this was the right place. I looked up at the sign which had been blown together. Instead of the two full names of the owners there was the name tallman. "Jimmy that's it! The tallman under the pyramid of light!" I exclaimed and almost started crying.

"Come on Parker, it's still open let's go," James urged and pulled me to the store.

"Oh my god, do you think this is it?" I asked as we pushed the door open.

We walked up to the counter and asked about the White Book. The clerk pointed to a shelf in the back of the store. We walked to the shelf and there it was like a shining beacon of hope.

I grabbed that book as if it were going to run out of the store on little legs. "Can I help you?" the clerk asked.

"Yeah, I'd like this book and this one," I said.

"Parker come on before the diner closes," James said and pulled me across the street.

We walked in the diner, Lou had his back to us when he said, "Sorry we're closed."

"Lou. I'm Parker and this is my very good friend James," I said.

He turned around and I thought he was going to faint. "You're the one I talked to. It's good to see you," he said and shook our hands.

"Come upstairs and I'll fix you something to eat. My grandparents live there are they in any danger?" Lou asked.

"No they aren't unless they go to her. Make sure they don't go near her until I say it's safe. Have you been prayin' for her?" I asked.

"Yes I have," Lou replied.

"Good just keep it up and she's gonna be fine I promise," I said.

We had a fantastic meal and as I was waiting for desert I started thumbing through the White Book. It wasn't a very big book and I'll be able to read it in no time. "Jimmy we're gonna have to get Marsh and Gracie's body together," I said.

"How are we gonna do that?" James asked and the faceless man appeared then it came to me, I knew exactly what I had to do.

I stood up, still holding the White Book. "You unimaginable bastard!" I hissed and a blast of white light flew out of me through the White Book and hit Quinn Larkwood, Marsh's father in the chest knocking him against the wall.

When Quinn hit the wall he was stuck there, then the four men dressed in white with the red crosses on their tunics arrived. "I'll deal with you later," I said as I walked up to him and pulled his face down so everyone could see it.

Sir Phillip appeared; he was dressed in the same clothing as the other four. "My Lady Parker I will make sure he is held in prison until you come for him," Sir Phillip said.

"Thank you Sir Phillip, thank you very much," I said and they disappeared.

"I'll answer the question that's on your minds, that's Marsh's father. He did this because he doesn't like me; her entire family is dead because of his actions. He helped Gracie to gain control, I don't know how yet but I'll find out."

"James to answer your question if she took the medicine I gave her she'll be out like a light so will Gracie. But I haven't been able to see her. I'm hopin' she's still bein' held at bay by," and I stopped.

"What is it?" James and Lou asked in unison.

"It's not my prayers, they're your prayers Lou. It says that whoever is takin' control of the body can be expelled only by the prayers of their one true love. Lou you've got to keep those prayers up. Has she been up here?" I asked.

"Yeah, she was and I had Clarice drive her to the bed and breakfast," Lou said and I shuddered.

"You need to go someplace that Marsh doesn't know about. We've got trouble it's as I thought. Gracie came back right after Marsh took the medicine I left for her. Gracie purged the medicine from Marsh's body before it could put her to sleep. She's on the way here, there's not a lot of time left," I said.

"We have a place we can go to. When should we go?" Lou asked.

Before I could answer James did. "Right now." I was kind of shocked; he did mention that he gets flashes. I just thought it was a line of bull so he could get me in bed. But I was wrong and the knock on the door proved it.

"Don't get it, it's her," James said. He went to the door and motioned for me to open it.

I opened it and there she stood, "Hello Gracie," I said. As she entered James did something to her and she dropped like a rock.

"Jimmy what did you do to her?" I asked. Secretly I wanted him to teach that move to me.

"No time to tell you about it. What do we do now?" James asked.

"We've got to keep her asleep. Lou you need to get your family out of here. Once they're safe call this number," I said and handed him my number.

"Parker why did you call me Jimmy? Only my uncle calls me that," he said.

"I don't know it just felt right. I won't do it again," I said.

"No that's alright," James said and smiled.

"How long will she be out?" I asked.

"For as long as need be," James said.

"Good, I need time to read the book," I said and sat down to read.

I found out what I needed to do to drive Gracie out of Marsh and destroy Gracie. I also found out how to contain Marsh's father. He would be imprisoned in a lead box, the box would have a lock and once locked there wouldn't be a key and couldn't be opened. I knew where it would be stored; it would be stored with the vast treasures housed under Briargate.

"Sir Phillip could you make a lead box four inches high, wide and deep with a lid and a lock but no key?" I asked

"Lady Parker it would be my great pleasure. Is this for him?" Sir Phillip asked.

"Yes it is, this is urgent so it will be needed as soon as possible. Can it be done quickly?" I asked.

"Yes Lady Parker it can be done quickly. I will make sure of it and I am going to start on it now," Sir Phillip said.

"Thank you very much Sir Phillip, I truly do appreciate it," I said.

"Jimmy I need to get Marsh to the crypt where Gracie is buried. Then the coffin has to be opened; the remains taken out and laid on a sheet of white that has been splashed with holy water."

"Once that's done Marsh has to be placed on a similar sheet, also splashed with holy water. Then a mirror has to be placed above Gracie's remains. When Gracie's spirit leaves Marsh's body and enters her own the mirror must be placed on top of Gracie's remains. It all has to be wrapped in the sheet and placed in the coffin."

"Once in the coffin, the mirror must be broken thus killing and holding Gracie's spirit throughout eternity," I said.

"How do we get Gracie out of Marsha?" James asked.

"Lou will stand by Gracie as he prays for Marsh, his prayers will draw her out. When Gracie is no more then I'll deal with Marsh's dad," I said.

I called Mom and gave her the list of supplies that I needed and where they needed to be taken to. I told her we would be leaving in a few hours and would be there as soon as possible. When I hung up I knew my worries were coming to an end. I also knew that everything I needed would be in the crypt when we got there.

Lou called, I told him that he needed to follow us and explained what he would have to do and he would have to be very brave and steady.

"Thank god we're here. The last one hundred miles felt like 10,000," I said and ran to the crypt to set everything up. I sprinkled the sheets with holy water, laid Gracie's remains on one table and Marsh on the other. James was able to rig up a system of wires and pulleys above Gracie's remains. When that was done he stood behind Lou and he started to pray.

I stood by Marsh and next to Lou. I took his hand and said, "Lou shut your eyes. Once we start to pray we can't stop. If you see Gracie come out it will startle you and if you stop even for a second it will be a disaster."

"Thank you Parker, thank you for everything," Lou said. He shut his eyes and we started to pray. I could see Gracie's spirit start to take shape and then she started to leave. She was being pulled to her remains by the prayers and the mirror. Her spirit entered her remains and her body started to begin to come back to life.

James stepped from behind the praying form of Lou and started to lower the mirror. When the mirror touched Gracie she started screaming and hitting the mirror. James wrapped the sheet over Gracie and the mirror. Then he secured it with several pieces of very strong plastic straps. When that was done he picked it up and placed it in the coffin.

Once that was done he took my position and I walked to the coffin, all the while praying and smashed the mirror. A shrill scream pierced the air and then it was silent.

"Hello Mr. Larkwood, Grandmother, Rosy, I'm glad you're here. Sir Phillip it's time," I said.

Sir Phillip arrived along with the box, the four men and the shackled form of Marsh's father. "Hello Parker, is it time to deal with this son of a bitch?" Mr. Larkwood asked.

"Yes it is," I said and Sir Phillip handed me the box.

The box had a lid that would detach and had four locks on it. "Would you raise him up?" I asked and his four guards raised him up.

They raised him up and I put the box below his feet. Then I put the lid above his head and started to push the lid down on his head. He started to plead and scream, but no amount of pleading and screaming would help him and then I ripped his mouth off and he could speak no more. "Save your breath, for your heinous actions your home will be this box from this day forward to eternity," I said as I continued to push until he was encased in his box. I put the lid on the box and locked all four locks.

"Sir Phillip can you take this home for me?" I asked.

"Lady Parker I would be honored to do so," Sir Phillip said and I handed him the box.

"Thank you very much," I said and they disappeared.

"We all want to thank you for eliminating a very large threat to the safety of everyone. How is my dear child?" Mr. Larkwood asked.

"You're very welcome. I would have moved heaven and earth to help Marsh. Physically she's fine, only time will tell about her state of mind," I replied.

"My dear child I'm so very proud of you," Grandmother said and wiped her eyes.

"Thank you Grandmother that means so very much to me," I said.

"Parker we must be off. Thank you once again from all of us," Mr. Larkwood said as he, Rosy and Grandmother smiled and they vanished.

"Parker," I said weakly and struggled to sit up.

"Marsh I'm so glad you're back," Parker said and hugged me.

"Lou," I said. Parker let go and stepped back so Lou and I could hold onto each other.

"Marsha I'm so happy you're alright," Lou said as he held me tight.

"James what's gonna happen to Marsh?" Parker asked.

"Well as far as I'm concerned she didn't do anything. I'm sure there won't be any evidence linking her to the murders. So I say let it alone," James said.

"That's what I was thinkin'. What about you two?" Parker asked as she slipped her hand into James' hand.

"I agree with you," Lou said.

"So do I," I said. Lou kissed my hand and I knew all was right with the world.

"Come on let's get out of here," Lou said as he led me out of the crypt. Parker stayed inside making sure everything was in order.

"Parker what's wrong? You should be thrilled," James said.

"I am and in a way I'm not. I'm still afraid for her. She won't be able to be alone for months to come. She will have to learn how to deal with this or she'll go crazy with grief," I said.

"Well you don't have anything to worry about. Lou will be with her and so will we," James said.

"What do you mean we?" I asked stupidly.

"Parker I'm here to help you and I will until forever comes. I like you very much besides that you smell good," James said and I thought I was going to die laughing.

"You really mean that don't you?" I asked.

"Yes I do," he replied.

"Well alright then, let's get out of here," I said and we joined Marsh and Lou.

The months went by and Marsh was the happiest I can ever remember seeing her. She was accepted by Lou's family as well as the entire town and soon they set their wedding date.

During these months there wasn't any mention of any of the people Gracie did away with and Marsh was doing extremely well. One day I was sitting in the stillness of the church when Marsh walked in, she didn't look very good.

She walked to where I was sitting and flung herself down next to me. "Parker," and she started sobbing.

"Marsh what's the matter?" I asked. Oh this wasn't good and I've worried about this for months now.

"I don't know. I just feel so miserable about what happened. Every time I look into Lou's eyes I see all the eyes of the lives I took. Oh Parker," Marsh cried and sobbed some more.

I grabbed Marsh by the shoulders and I shook her. "Marsha stop it right now! Do you understand me? You didn't do it. You're gonna marry a wonderful man who loves you more than life itself. So get a grip," I said and hugged Marsh.

The wedding was magnificent; I was so proud of Marsh. She pulled herself together and was more beautiful than ever, she looked like a princess. Her shiny deep green eyes sparkled with joy; we put just a little makeup on her high cheek bones to hide the scars that were already fading. For one of the few times we managed to tame that curly mass of honey brown hair by braiding it with strands of fine silver and gold with tiny jewels embedded on them. Marsh and Lou went on a beautiful and well deserved honeymoon which was exactly what they both needed.

While they were gone I went back to Briargate with James. The first thing I did when I arrived was to retrieve the box that held Marsh's father. I welded the lid shut then sacred and blessed runes were carved on the lid and on the bottom of the box. The runes were also carved along the welded seam, thus sealing him in. I also affixed sacred, blessed stones on the lid and in between the runes that sealed the lid. With this done, I was satisfied Marsh's father would be secure in his prison, never to cause harm to anyone ever again. I placed the box in a very special, very secure area where no one will ever find him.

I received a phone call from Marsh saying they were making a stop in London and of course they were coming to stay at Briargate. When we picked them up Marsh looked absolutely fabulous, so did Lou, but I saw a black cloud surrounding her. I'm also very sure that the news I have for her will perk her right up.

Marsh and I went for a long walk and I showed her the sights. I forgot about my ring, it wasn't a huge thing just a beautiful band of brushed gold. "Parker when did you and James get married?"

"A month before you and Lou did," I said.

"Why didn't you tell me?" Marsh asked.

"Because we didn't want to rain on your parade. After all you had been through you deserved to be the center of attention," I said and smiled. This was a smile Marsh hasn't seen in quite a while; Marsh knew I had some big news for her.

"Well I wanted to be there, like we had always planned," Marsh said.

"Marsh don't get your panties in a bind. We were plannin' to have a church wedding when we got back to the states and you're gonna be my maid of honor," Parker said.

"Well okay then. Alright Parker spill the beans I know what that smile means," Marsh said, she couldn't stand it any longer.

"Well how have you been feelin' lately?" I asked; Marsh just looked at me.

"Well I've been feelin' a little queasy the last couple of weeks. I just chalked it up to the excitement of the wedding, the honeymoon, traveling and all the different foods we've been eating," Marsh said and I started to laugh.

"Oh god Marsh it's none of the above. You really don't know do you?" I asked.

"No I don't, I have no clue what you're talkin' about," Marsh said.

"You're pregnant!" I exclaimed and wrapped Marsh up in a hug.

"I'm what?" Marsh stammered; she just couldn't wrap her head around that information.

"Pregnant. PREGNANT does that help it sink in any better for you?" I asked. I was so happy for her, Marsh started to cry for joy and the blackness around her was gone, it was replaced by a brilliant gold aura.

"Oh Parker I'm so happy!" Marsh exclaimed and we latched on to each other.

When Marsh was finally able to get her emotions in check she said, "You know I'm gonna have to get one of those tests before I tell Lou."

"You don't need to buy any I've got an extra one at the house. No I'm not yet, I thought I was but I'm not. So come on let's go!" I exclaimed. We ran back to Briargate and made a bee line to the bathroom.

Marsh came out of the bathroom test stick in hand. She shoved it almost completely in my face, sure enough there was a blue positive just as I told her. Marsh looked at me, I nodded my head and Marsh went running down the stairs yelling, "Lou! Lou! Where are you?"

Lou came running; he had a look of pure panic on his face. "Oh my god Marsha are you hurt? What's wrong?"

"Lou, Lou nothin', look, look!" Marsh exclaimed and shoved the test stick at him; he looked at it and didn't have a clue.

When Lou didn't respond Marsh ever so softly said, "I'm pregnant."

"You want to tell me that again. Pregnant," and it ever so slowly started to sink in.

"Yeah pregnant," Marsh said and started to cry.

"Oh Marsha, I'm so damn happy," Lou said, picked her up, hugged her and buried his face in her neck.

As the days and weeks passed my growing belly proclaimed to the world that I was bringing new life into it. Lou and I were over the moon happy and I was told by several people that I was glowing! James and Parker were there for the birth of my beautiful baby girl. Parker later told me she had never seen two people so happy and radiant. My pregnancy was the best thing for me, I now have a daughter to love and care for; all negative thoughts of what Gracie did to me were gone.

James and Parker were there when Maryella Parker Spagtini came into the world, man oh man did Parker have a fit when I told her I was going to give my daughter her first name as her middle name. She went on and one about it but in the end she smiled and gave me her blessing. I knew she would, she just had to blow herself out. So anyway James and Parker were there to welcome Maryella into the world and then see her christened. I wanted Clarice and Parker both to be Maryella's godmothers and James to be the godfather which they all jumped at the chance.

A couple of months after Maryella's birth James and Parker had to return to Briargate. "Parker are you sure you're okay to fly?" I asked and rubbed Parker's ever expanding pregnant belly.

"Yeah my doctor said I was okay but not for much longer. We're both hopin' we'll be able to take care of business and come back here sooner than later," Parker said as she rubbed her back.

James and Parker left the next day and it was very hard for both of us. "Parker I'm gonna miss you so bad. Please take care of yourself and if you need anything don't hesitate to call me, you know I'll be there for you as fast as I can get there," I said and her deep violet eyes were red and filled with tears, well so were mine.

"Marsh I'm so proud of you. Ever since you married Lou and now with Maryella you've become a new, more confident and powerful woman. You're a force to contend with and I'm so happy you're my sister. If I need anything you my sister will be the first one I call," Parker said and we hugged not wanting to let go.

One month after Parker and James left, Parker went into labor; three weeks early. Lou and I were running around like chickens with our heads cut off trying to get everything together. We were going to leave Maryella with Al, Maria and Clarice; mind you they were thrilled to death to watch her. "Come on Marsha we've got to go, we're gonna be late!" Lou called.

"I'm comin'; I'm comin' hold your pants we've got plenty of time. Now Maryella you mind your Nanna," I said and Maria started to laugh because Maryella was only four months old.

"Marsha my dear you're a love. Now you get goin' before Lou picks you up and carries you out of here," Maria said and hugged me, then I hugged Al; out the door I ran and jumped into the truck.

"Lou look out!" I screamed.

"Marsha!" I screamed and dropped to her knees.

"Parker what's wrong baby?" Jimmy asked and dropped down next to me.

"Jimmy, Lou and Marsh were in a terrible accident! They're both alive but Marsh is in unbelievably bad shape! She used up most of her strength keepin' Lou from goin' into the light before his time!" I cried and James bundled me up in his strong arms.

"Parker," Marsh called.

"Marsh you get back in your body! You've got a baby to raise and I'll be darned if I'm gonna lose you! We are gonna grow old together!" I ordered and Marsh slammed back into her body.

Four months after the accident I was finally able to travel with my baby boys. Our first stop was Mom and Dad so they could baby sit for us. James and I made our way to the hospital, I made my way to Marsh's bed, took her hand and kissed her. "Oh my sister, you have so many people here waitin' for you. Please come back, Lou and Maryella need you," I said.

"Parker my beloved sister. I know they do but I'm not strong enough yet. It took so much out of me when I saved Lou. I'm still so very tired but I'm growin' stronger every day. Parker I promise I'll come back. Tell Lou I love him and give Maryella a kiss for me," Marsh said and walked off with Mr. Larkwood. Marsh turned around and gave me a wave and then Mr. Larkwood and Marsh went into his house.

"Parker are you alright?" Lou asked. I hadn't realized I had tears streaming down my face.

"Yeah Lou I am. Marsh says she loves you and she'll be back. She's very tired and not strong enough yet but she said she's comin' back. She also wants me to give Maryella a kiss for her," I said and wiped my eyes and kissed Maryella.

"Parker do you know when she'll come back?" Lou asked and wiped his tears away.

"I don't know, someday, someday," I said and looked down at my sister who lay in a deep, deep coma.

www.ingramcontent.com/pod-product-compliance
Lightning Source LLC
Chambersburg PA
CBHW021013160726
47994CB00006B/2499